Pay the Price and Other Stories

Larry I. Samuels

Pay the Price and Other Stories

Copyright © 2014 by Larry I. Samuels

ISBN-13: 978-0615973890

First Edition

The Steam Press

P.O. Box # 82
Worton, MD 21678

thesteampress@gmail.com

"Gasoline Alley" and "Puke" originally published in *A Potpourri of Prose and Poetry* by the Chestertown Writers Group, Copyright © 2013. Used with acknowledgement to Little Bear Press.

Dedication

This collection is gratefully dedicated to my dear wife Marguerite Anne, who is an insightful writer, a superb editor, wonderful teacher, loving mother, friendly and respected aunt, the encouraging shelter of our family, and influences so much of what I do in life; and to my children Paul Henry and Rebecca Marie who patiently indulge me as I continue to talk to them occasionally in seafaring terms.

A special thanks to members of the Chestertown Writers Group who provided the catalyst to pursue this work.

Pay the Price and Other Stories
Table of Contents

Introduction by Author	i - vii
Gasoline Alley	1 - 22
Taxicab Rides	23 - 58
Class "A" School	59 - 72
Six & Six	73 - 86
Puke	87 - 102
Liberty Call	103 - 128
Olongapo City	129 - 158
Tattoo	159 - 174
Crossing Over	175 - 180
Jewel of the East	181 - 192
She Had to Leave and They Couldn't Talk	193 - 208
Amusement Parks	209 - 222
After Schoolwork	223 - 240
Pay the Price	241 - 270
About the Author	271 - 276
Appendix	277 - 286

Pay the Price & Other Stories
Introduction

I have been writing short stories on and off for most of the past more than fifty some-odd years, ever since I started by pounding on my aunt's manual typewriter – a vintage 1950s Remington model with a combination black and red ribbon. One of my earliest stories was about a trip to the moon, and when the crew came back to earth, they mysteriously died. Just some light fare by an eleven year-old. Wish I still had a copy of that story – I could perform some editing, to make it a bit grimmer. Well, that's what happens after one re-reads what one has written – sometimes it comes back to haunt you.

That is the task of writing. You need to work hard at getting things right, and sometimes things go wrong rather easily. This has been the case for me in so many areas – with my family in the big city, going to school, having many diverse jobs, in romantic encounters, while serving in the U.S. Navy, marrying, having two children, etc. That is the nature of life - getting things right and getting things wrong. While these experiences have obviously been uniquely mine, they are also universal in one form or another.

My writing has been like that, unique and universal. Capturing in writing what are my own stories, but disguising them in a fictional voice, anticipating them to appeal to all readers, or to a specific audience.

Other writers do it that way, and perhaps more so in order to appeal to a targeted group. This is especially true since one is supposed to write about what one knows, and that would help to focus on to whom you are writing.

I guess I think that I know some things about writing, but maybe not enough, since I have only taken one formal adult creative writing class to help me improve my writing.

It did help. And what also helped was to write fiction without stopping – you must keep plugging away. In addition, I was fortunate in my work career to have the responsibility to produce tomes of business reports, grant applications, environmental studies, construction specifications, and correspondence – kept me writing non-fiction, though creatively, and correctly.

I also joined a friendly writers group two years ago for the informal critique and camaraderie that it provided, and was inspired to resurrect and edit several previous fictional works, and to write many new pieces. My joining the writers group led to the most exciting thing that could happen to a writer, in my opinion – publication. The members, along with my wife who also joined us, were able to self-publish an eclectic collection of prose and poetry in paperback, for sale and for inclusion in our local county public library and bookstore – it was thrilling.

The stories in this current collection of mine basically revolve around the times before, during, and after my service in the U.S. Navy. I tried to capture what it was like in those times, as a civilian before I enlisted, and as a sailor during the war in Vietnam.

I describe being on board ships as I was deep within the engineering spaces, or while I was on the beach, on liberty or leave, and afterward when separated from active duty. The stories involve protagonists and characters that have experienced being in these varieties of situations against the background of historical cultural events.

Besides in this collection that I depict a composite form of myself as the main character, or as other characters, some of these accounts involve persons other than myself which could be me, or involve characters that are not me. After all, this is a marginally fictionalized collection. Most of this is true except for what really happened.

Although I was on a ship in the Gulf of Tonkin in the "Blue Water" Navy and did not have to face the overwhelmingly horrifying aspects of ground combat nor did I have the experience of running patrol boats near the shore or on rivers, the "Brown Water" Navy, we destroyer sailors had our share of uncertainties and danger.

Basically, we were shelling the Viet Cong or otherwise providing gunfire support for U.S. Marine ground operations with our main 5" diameter gun, and could also provide missile fire. The enemy was also shooting back at us, either with conventional guns, or they could get to us with other weapon systems. Sometimes we got in too close to the shore, less than the usual approximately 20,000 yards offshore at the edge of the gun's firing range, and took some shrapnel, but mostly we didn't.

We also steamed full ahead at a screaming, roaring speed greater than twenty-five knots to provide plane guarding for the aircraft carriers from the flight decks of which Navy pilots were flying over Vietnam.

The planes were landing on the carriers as they returned from firing on the enemy. Sometimes the pilots didn't make it back, but mostly they did. We never did have to rescue any pilots, but we could have.

Not to be presumptuous, though thinking along these lines, I was modeling this collection on James A. Michener's short stories *Tales of the South Pacific,* concerning his service in the Navy during World War II, as he wished to describe what it was actually like, as he himself notes in the lead story. This comparison of my writing to his is a pretty tall order indeed for an author of my present stature, but it can't hurt to try.

Some of his stories in that collection included several of the same characters in each of them, either actually named or otherwise alluded to. It worked pretty well for him, and I almost did something like that in this collection, although not quite. After all, I'm not James A. Michener, just an admirer.

Nor did I have anywhere near the hideous experiences of another extremely strong writer of Vietnam war stories, who included several repeating characters, Tim O'Brien, especially in his collection, *The Things They Carried,* a shocking and compelling display of war and personal trials.

There are any number of other superb collections of war stories, covering the human elements in conflicts beginning from antiquity, as well as more contemporary prose describing, for example, the two World Wars, Korea, Vietnam, and beyond. I cannot begin to name the wealth of literature available on these themes.

It's just that some of my stories parallel the universal experience of being involved in war, or of experiencing military service in general, and the enveloping environment of that world.

My experiences during the four years that I served in the Navy were at the same time both extraordinary and trivial. I know that I share these feelings with veterans of all branches of the armed forces, along with the often heard generally amazing statement made by many while on active duty, "Hey, what am I doing here?"

This view seems almost universal among military personnel – hopefully, at least to those not completely devastated or horribly disabled, either physically, mentally, or emotionally by their service experiences. It is one thing to have a neutral or positive experience in the military and obviously quite another to have been maimed or paralyzed, or to have died, or to have lost someone to war. The amazement of being in war is a reaction to being in a completely unique situation far from home or otherwise having to face conditions that lack anything resembling a familiar previous experience, and it's dangerous.

It's even called out in that great novelty song of 1960 recorded by Larry Verne, "Mr. Custer," about that fateful day in the life of the U.S. Army's 7th Cavalry's fighting against the Sioux at the Little Big Horn.

One lone soldier, while surveying the situation with the enemy all around him, rings out loud and clear with that very statement, and then asks his sergeant in a trembling voice if he can be excused for the rest of the afternoon. A vivid testament to military awe, uncertainty, and irreverence so precisely captured.

On the other hand, besides as a reaction to adversity, one might make this statement of wonderment as an expression of total astonishment that one is actually in some fabled place of the world which one may never have had the opportunity to visit, if it hadn't been for serving in a branch of the military. Either way, it can be overwhelming.

As I constructed these stories, I was also mindful of another great collection that I have read and admire describing naval service, Richard McKenna's, *The Left-Handed Monkey Wrench*. His stories of ship-board life while serving as a steam plant engineer, and of his shore duty adventures in the Far East during the early twentieth century, along with his monumental novel, *The Sand Pebbles,* were fertile examples for my striving to emulate this author. Both Michener's and McKenna's writings depict exciting and mundane experiences that are full of the triumphs and pathos of human interactions. That's how I view my stories – if I didn't see them that way, there would be no point in presenting them.

These stories of mine also provide entertainment and technical information, both as personal narratives and as travelogues. There are emotions and practical details in these stories that should make readers feel uplifted, sad, thoughtful, and informed.

As I have stated, some of these stories are set in the time before my service in the Navy, some take place against the background of active duty, and some describe the time following my Honorable Discharge from the military.

They all have the purpose of presenting a picture of situations and people that shape or otherwise change one's personality, that describe topical events, and which include life's triumphs, mistakes, oversights, and improvements. It is my anticipation that the reader will find these qualities in this collection.

March 20, 2011 – February 21, 2015

Pay the Price and Other Stories

Gasoline Alley

The rubber hose clanged the service bell twice –
someone had driven over it completely up to the first gas
pump. "I'll get it," Vincent said to Willy, the other service
attendant on this shift.

Vincent got up from the chair that was set just
outside of the gas station office, tugged at the rag sticking
out of the back pocket of his green uniform and walked
directly to the driver's side of the red and white four-door
'57 Plymouth Plaza. It was 1969.

The guy driving it said, "Fill it up, please; regular."
Sometimes they said please, sometimes they didn't. This
wasn't much of a concern to Vincent. He would pump gas
for them whether they asked nicely or not. He walked
around the back of the car, opened the fuel door, lifted the
hose nozzle, started the pump, placed the nozzle in the
funnel, squeezed the handle and flipped the automatic
holder to the last setting. It would click off when the tank
was nearly full.

He took the squeegee from the bucket of water at
the end of the pump island and sponged the windshield
wet, then cleaned it off with the rubber blade. "Check your
oil?" he asked the driver. "Yeah, sure," he answered.

The hood was held open by hydraulic arms. He
pulled the dipstick out, wiped it off, placed it back and
pulled it out. He could see from the glistening oil film that
the level was within range, and not too dirty. The fuel
pump clicked off.

1

"Oil's good," he said out loud. He walked over to the pump and squeezed the handle again to top off the tank at what was usually a dead-on even-dollar amount, or at a five or ten-cent increment. He didn't often miss.

"That'll be $7.50," he said. It was about twelve gallons. The driver pulled out his wallet and handed Vincent a five dollar bill, and three singles. "Keep the change, buddy," he said. That was a treat – sometimes they tipped, mostly not. And for fifty-cents this time, not too bad. Usually it would be a quarter, if anything. "Thanks, pal," Vincent answered. The guy started his car and drove out of the station, clanging over the next hose, into a relatively light traffic pattern. It was just past 10:00 p.m. *One more hour, Vincent thought, then I'm out of here.*

He walked back to his chair and sat down, but didn't feel a need to say anything to Slim Willy sitting next to him. Willy was a friendly family man, a nice guy to work with, who knew the score. He was shorter than Vincent, wiry, and still spoke with a southern drawl carried from his being born and raised in Georgia.

Vincent and Willy got along very well – Vincent got along with most everyone. Some nights he worked with Willy, some nights with his other partner, Big Bill, an affable gentleman in his late forties, way street smart.

Big Bill had a long, dark scar across the back of his neck, the remains of a long-ago card game that had gone very wrong. Bill was a gigantic, thick man, standing well over 6'-5" and strong, capable of effortlessly lifting heavy wheels onto the pneumatic machine to break down tires from rims to fix flats.

2

Vincent was only slightly feeling the strain of walking back and forth from this evening's work. Standing 5'-9" and stocky, with thick curly black hair and medium-length sideburns, he had brown eyes and a clean-shaven, friendly face. He could work for long periods of time, but he was feeling just a little tired this night.

He had been working at this service station on Coney Island Avenue in Brooklyn, New York for about a year and a half. He came in at 5:00 p.m. and worked until he closed at 11:00 p.m., five nights a week. At least he didn't have to work on the weekends – that was great. Willy and Bill shared alternate weekends with two other employees that Vincent would sometimes run into.

This weeknight job was after school. He was attending a local community college, majoring in the preliminary courses required for a two-year Associates Degree in Liberal Arts.

At this point in his life he really didn't have much direction after being graduated from high school two years before. He was attending college to avoid the military draft, with the prospect of being shipped directly to Vietnam if he did get drafted.

He was fortunate to be working these hours. He could still attend school and he was making money. At the hourly rate of $1.75, he was making $ .50 per hour above the current minimum wage. He was always in cigarette money, could buy gas for his car and could entertain dates.

He was living at home with his father, mother, two sisters and a brother, and had secured a student loan to pay for books. He was fortunate that at this time tuition was free at this municipal college.

He had turned eighteen after high school, and had registered for the draft. He held a 2-S deferment classification as a college student, however, this would change to 1-A status, ready for induction, if he left school. It was pretty elitist to provide draft deferments for college students, but that was the contemporary landscape.

Deferments were also being provided for teachers – a more noble enterprise. Some men were also getting draft deferments for essential work, at hospital power plants for instance.

Once his classification would change if he left school, it could likely be just a matter of time when he would be drafted into the Army to serve in Vietnam. Not a good situation.

He had a cousin in the Marine Corps that had been wounded in Vietnam during the Tet Offensive a year before in 1968 at Khe Sanh, the base located in the district capital of Quang Tri province. It was an overwhelming and horrifying time for his cousin, the family, and friends. His cousin had recovered, but the entire family had been distraught.

They were now facing the possibility of this happening again to a family member, or a worse possibility, if Vincent would go over.

His leaving school, if he did, would start the clock on his induction. It wasn't a certainty that he would go straight to Vietnam, but it was a very distinct possibility.

He wasn't that gung-ho about putting himself in the situation of being in the military in order to defend his country. His patriotism was indistinct and not a priority for him.

There was no tradition in his family of especially noteworthy military service, just the obligatory World War II involvement experienced by his father, and several uncles, and the wounding of his cousin. It didn't seem to him that he needed to be in the direct line of fire to have to live up to any ideal or to prove anything to anyone.

Completing a standard regulation stint in the military would suffice for his personal satisfaction. He would be in conformance with what he believed to be customary behavior within his socio-economic class.

He wasn't, however, overly intellectual about all of this. As far as military service, he wasn't against it at all, even in these dangerous times during the war of ground combat and extreme negativity towards the military – and extreme support. These were the days of "Hawks" and "Doves," of the philosophy, "America, Love It, or Leave It." He could see that there were benefits to having military training and experience.

It would mean being able to take advantage of the GI Bill for Education and of a Veteran's Administration Home Loan – he could see all that.

His father had gone to school after WW II and had used his VA loan to buy their first house. There were positive aspects of military service; however, one had to live through the experience to make that work. Although he could see the benefits, he only wanted to limit the extent of catastrophic circumstances that he might encounter. While military service seemed to be honorable, it certainly didn't have to include direct combat in Vietnam.

The purpose of the war in Vietnam was fairly obscure to him. It wasn't talked about at all in any of his classes throughout junior high school or high school during the mid-to-late sixties – not that he had experienced these academic exercises, anyway. They did learn about world history in school, however.

European history, that is, and not too much ever about Asia or Africa, of which he didn't remember learning a whole lot about that area of the world, except for the part about European colonization.

Because the war was all around him, he did think that he might eventually be very involved in it. He wasn't particularly affected, however, by the major protests against the war going on at the time, almost all of which seemed to be by college students.

Vietnam Veterans themselves, however, were also starting to make statements against the war. His politics, though, were not in alignment with any movement. None of his friends were talking about the war, only about how they were hoping to avoid being drafted.

During those times when the war was on, job candidates were being asked by prospective employers during interviews just what was their draft status. Companies weren't too keen on hiring and then training people who would potentially have to go into the military. It was difficult for males of draft age who had some vision of their career paths to be able to focus on their plans, with the possible disruption of their lives beckoning them in the near future. It was a very real dilemma in relation to general employment, not to mention the obvious doubts about actual survival, or if one would physically or mentally remain whole, if one went into combat.

This kind of job analysis didn't apply to Vincent's employment as a gas station attendant while still in school. He hadn't been asked about his draft status when he was hired to pump gas. His uncle had worked at this gas station two years before Vincent, and the owner had been satisfied when he had vouched for Vincent as an honest, hard-working man. He was safe in school and at the station for the time being. The looming specter of Vietnam was still in the future as long as he stayed in school.

For Vincent, and so many other young men at the time, the war was so pervasive in all aspects of work life and culture that its effects were devastating, though obviously not in any way at the same level of destruction as what the active military personnel were experiencing.

Slim Willy and Big Bill were way past draft age, both black men in their forties, and Army veterans of World War II.

Vincent was much younger, and white. They all got along famously. As he had heard from his father about war service, Vincent was interested to learn about their service during the war, although they didn't talk about it much.

As far as his getting along in this racially mixed environment, he had been raised in a very progressive and tolerant household and had always been hustling work since his early teens, getting along with people of various nationalities.

Not that he was actively involved in any way with the Civil Rights movement, but he couldn't understand the appalling culture of racism in the country, and did experience a terrible and deep sense of loss the year before in April of 1968 when he heard over the radio that Dr. Martin Luther King, Jr. had been assassinated in Memphis, Tennessee.

He knew the country would never be the same after losing this giant leader, just like it had never really recovered from the assassination of President John F. Kennedy in November of 1963, and of Senator Robert F. Kennedy in June of 1968. Between the war and social unrest, these were turbulent and uncertain times.

But Vincent wasn't thinking much about these things as he sat with Willy waiting for the next customer. It didn't become too busy during the next hour at work. A few cars came in, no flat tires to fix, and he and Willy shared in pumping gas.

About 10:45 p.m., Vincent started to close up. He took a clipboard with a chart from its hook on a wall in the office and read the meters on the fuel pumps.

He went into the service garage and to the electrical panel, shutting down the circuit breakers for the pumps, and the flood lights. He counted the money in the cash register, placed the few credit card charge slips together and placed all of that in an empty plastic juice pitcher. He tucked the pitcher into a space on one of the shelves in the supply closet in the back of the office.

It was Frank's idea, the station owner, who thought keeping the night receipts casually like that in the shop was a lot safer than having Vincent as the night manager walk it to the bank depository. Frank would be coming in the next morning to open up and to check Vincent's accounting. Frank would make whatever bank deposit he needed to make.

He trusted Vincent, and Vincent really had a lot of responsibility at his age.

Vincent and Willy changed out of their coverall uniforms into street clothes. Vincent shut out the office lights and locked the door. They said goodnight to each other and Willy jumped into to his 1963 four-door Pontiac Bonneville Safari station wagon.

Not a particularly special vehicle, but for Willy and his wife and four children, it was good transportation. The trouble was that Willy's car usually had a few cockroaches in it – the result of his bringing various bags full of clothes and other items to the car from his house, which also had cockroaches.

These transports and the habit that Willy had of always eating in his car – this kept the cockroaches happy. Willy never complained about this condition.

Vincent never did find out how Willy's family felt about it – he guessed they were just used to it.

Closing up, now it was time for Vincent to grab a bite to eat. The nearest places for food were about a half-mile down the avenue. It was either at "George's," a coffee shop and luncheonette, or the almost-famous "Big Daddy's," a "Nathan's Famous" type hot dog, hamburger, French fries and beer joint with a parking lot.

Besides various eateries, this section of Coney Island Avenue, and most of the rest of it, from Bartel-Pritchard Square at the northern entrance of Prospect Park, about two miles away, and to the south, ending some five miles later at Brighton Beach Avenue on the edge of Coney Island, almost exclusively contained other gas stations at approximately two block intervals.

Crammed in between the stations were car repair shops, used car lots, new car dealerships, tire shops, car washes, auto glass replacement shops, car sound system installation shops, foreign and domestic auto parts stores, junk yards, cab companies, car insurance offices, and car and truck rental companies, all on a major bus route – this was gasoline alley.

Vincent got into his car, a steel gray '61 Chevrolet Bel Air, two-door sedan. Big eight cylinders, 283 cubic inch engine, weighed just under 3,500 pounds.

A really great automobile. Although it sold for about $2,600 as new in 1961, now these eight years later he had scraped together the $625 he had paid for it from his savings while working all during high school at the corner candy store, helping his father and mother run the house.

He had always worked, delivering orders for the local butcher shop, or at one of the neighborhood grocery stores packing orders. He had delivered dry cleaning for a neighborhood store after school and managed the Laundromat next door to that for three nights during the week, and on weekends. He always had a few dollars in his pocket.

Being employed at the gas station gave him the opportunity to work on his Chevrolet as necessary – not that it really needed a lot of work at this time. Even though it had almost 100,000 miles on it, he could keep it tuned up, changing spark plugs, points, condenser, oil and filter, keeping the engine timed, replacing brakes, like that. It was good to be on gasoline alley.

He drove to "Big Daddy's." Parking, then going to the counter, he ordered a hamburger, French fries and a soda. He sat at one of the outdoor tables, ate, and then smoked a cigarette. It was getting late and he had an early class the next morning. Although he sometimes almost slept through the early ones, he wasn't doing too badly at school, maintaining about a B average. He just needed to stick it out until he could figure out what he was going to do about the situation with school versus the draft.

Without a career direction, he wasn't really satisfied staying there in school, but wasn't exactly ready yet to enlist in the Navy, an option that he had been considering. Joining up would end the uncertainty of the draft.

That next night, Vincent was back at work, pumping gas, gauging oil, checking water, cleaning windshields, basically relaxed, and not unhappy.

He was working with Bill tonight. The conversation between them was lively and full of stories about pool halls, traveling down south and meeting women. Bill liked to talk, and Vincent could keep up with him.

About 9:00 p.m., a dark blue '65 Mustang fast-back with white-wall tires pulled in. Sitting there behind the steering wheel was a dark-haired woman wearing a tee-shirt and a cut-off dungaree jacket.

The rock music from her radio was turned up loud. She turned it off, and shut down the engine. To Vincent, she looked a few years older than him.

He walked over, leaned down to her face, looked directly into her blue eyes, and said evenly, "Can I help you, miss?"

She looked up at him for a moment, and said, "I need a fill-up, high test. She continued to look at him, hard. "Then I need you to check my front." Vincent didn't blink – for some reason she had clearly found an immediate connection just by looking at him.

"Sure, I can take care of that for you." He was only slightly thinking about pumping gas. He was, however, thinking about filling her tank, so to speak.

He went over to the pump, opened the fuel door at the rear of the car, and started putting in the gas. He walked to the front of her car, and smiled into the windshield. She smiled back. He lifted the hood and checked the fluids. Oil, radiator, power steering, and brake fluids were fine.

The pump clicked off. He was going to make sure he clicked back on with her. He stopped the pump, walked around to her side, leaned down and said, "It came to $5.00."

Then he continued, "By the way, nice ride you've got here, nice paint color, great engine, that 289 V-8. I know you can move pretty fast in this car. Anything else I can do for you?"

He liked what he saw here. His wheels were spinning fast to what he hoped would be the very near future. Whatever she was going to say next, he was going to say something clever to follow that up, maybe to get the chance to keep this going.

"Well, I don't need anything else right now," she said. "I have to be somewhere tonight, soon. You like this car? So do I. It fits me real good, like a glove. I like things that have a nice fit."

To Vincent, there was no mistaking what she was talking about. Although Vincent was no slouch when it came to dating, and sex, this exchange was going as fast as that Mustang of hers could go.

They were racing together at top speed.

Before he could say anything else, she said, "I've been driving this car solid since I bought it last year. Let me get some money out of my handbag."

She stretched over to the passenger side, real slowly. He watched as her jeans inched down a little over her shapely behind. He was impressed.

She handed him a ten-dollar bill. "You keep the change, honey," she said. "I'm going to start gassing up here from now on. It's worth it for good service. I'll be back real soon when I need more."

"Sure thing. My name's Vincent Salmon. What's yours?" he asked

"I'm Jane. Jane Bennett. Nice to meet you, Vincent. Thanks for the gas."

"No, thank you for your gift – you're now one of my best customers, and the nicest looking." He had come up with something sharp to say.

"You're sweet," she smiled at him as she started the car, and stepped hard on the accelerator, burning a little rubber while she pulled out. He watched as she drove out of the station and onto the street. *Would she be back the next night?* He certainly felt like she would, and hoped so, and then he had the electric expectation that she would be there. Difficult to explain, just one look like that, but it happened sometimes, especially in 1969.

Bill said, "Hey boy, what was that all about? Looked like you were checking out more than her oil."

"Oh, yeah, something going on there. Nice looking car, nice looking driver – I hope I'll be filling her up with something real soon."

Bill laughed. "Good luck, buddy, fine young thing there in that fine car. Thinking about that, I think I'll see my girlfriend tonight."

"You take it easy, Bill, don't strain your old self."

Bill laughed even harder. "Don't worry about me, kid, I can handle it. Hope you can."

Vincent closed the station at 11:00 p.m. He would be working with Bill the next night as well.

Bill drove off in his car, a throaty-sounding 1960, two-door Ford Galaxie, with reflectors on the mud flaps hanging behind the rear wheels.

Instead of "Big Daddy's" Vincent hit the coffee shop for a bacon, lettuce, and tomato sandwich on rye toast, with a cup of coffee. Then he went home to wait until tomorrow.

It was about 10:00 p.m. the next night. He had not had any classes that day. He was sitting in his chair outside of the office with Bill. The blue Mustang pulled in alongside the pump island. Vincent got up and walked over to greet her.

"Hi, Jane, how's it going?"

"I'm fine, you okay?"

"Yeah, I'm good. What can I get for you?"

"Nothing here, I don't need any gas since yesterday. But there's something you can help me with at my house." She was looking right at him and he was looking right back at her.

"Happy to oblige. You're just in time. Let me close up here and change my clothes. I'll be right with you."

"Why don't you just close, and you can change at my house?"

Even this was fast for Vincent. "Sure, I'll be right with you. Why don't you just pull over to the other side of this island?" She moved the car away from the pumps and left the motor running. Vincent walked back to Bill.

"I guess I know what you're doing tonight," Bill said.

"As soon as we get out of here, looks like my ship has come in," Vincent answered.

He took the readings, counted out, put the money away, and grabbed his change of clothes. Bill said, "So long, see you sometime," and left the shop. Vincent shut the lights, and locked the door. Although somewhat distracted, his concentration on what needed to be done at the station was not debatable.

Vincent opened the passenger side door of her car and got in. "My car is parked on the street around the corner," he said.

"It'll keep until tomorrow," she said. "I don't live too far from here."

"I'm all yours," he answered.

"Yes you are," she said. He was feeling fine – this was nothing like he had been involved with before.

They drove north on the avenue for about five minutes, past one of the entrances to Prospect Park, then a few blocks farther.

She parked on the street near a three-story brownstone apartment building. This section of Coney Island Avenue was all residential, with only the occasional grocery store or pizza parlor facing the park.

They walked to the building entrance, not talking. She was several inches shorter than him. She was wearing black slacks, white sneakers and a tee-shirt, accented with her dungaree jacket.

Although he had partially seen what she looked like in her car, the street light revealed that she was indeed a good-looking woman with a trim figure, dark blue eyes and a bright, forthright look on her face. Vincent was feeling pretty good.

"Here we are," she said, as she opened the apartment door on the second floor. She turned on a light in the hall, and led him to the living room.

She turned on a lamp, and said, "Why don't you sit down and I'll fix us a couple of drinks. I have gin – how's that?"

"Nice, thanks." He sat on the couch, a little hesitantly, considering that he was still in his work clothes, and placed his street clothes on the floor. He looked around the room. A television set, two modern easy chairs, a glass coffee table in front of the couch, an area rug and the end table with the lamp. He could see the bedroom off to the left.

She came back into the living room carrying two drinks. Handing him one of them, she sat down next to him.

"Cheers," she said.

"Here's to you, babe."

They took a sip, and then Jane said, "You probably want to get out of those work clothes, don't you?"

"I could change," he said. "Let me go into the bathroom."

"Don't bother, Vincent, why not just take them off here? I need to get out of my clothes, too."

Although up to this point, ever since the other night when they had first met, and Jane had come on to him, they had not spoken much about anything except small talk of what, and how each of them was doing, and some car comments. It didn't seem to matter. She, and he, just had one thing on their minds, and it was going to happen.

They helped each other strip out of their clothes in the living room, then she led him to the bedroom. It was dreamy and frenzied.

Jane woke up first the next morning, and then she woke him.

"Vincent, I need to get to work." She had told him last night that she was the bookkeeper for a small manufacturing company in downtown Brooklyn. She had been working there about three years.

Before that, she had worked for a lighting supply company, also as a bookkeeper, following graduation from high school. She was twenty-seven years old.

"Sorry to see you go," he said. "It was great last night."

"Sure was, you got my motor running in high gear."

"Glad to be of service," he said.

She jumped into the shower. Vincent followed soon after; then they had coffee, and buttered toast. They mostly talked about cars, and engine displacements, and accessories. They left the apartment together. Jane dropped Vincent off at his car.

"Maybe I'll see you tonight," he said.

"Maybe you will," she said. "If not, I'll be around sometime."

"Looking forward to it," he said.

She didn't make it the next night. But she did come around to the station every few nights after that, during the next three months. Willy and Bill thought it was really hot, this arrangement that Vincent had with this woman.

It was always the same. She would pick him up around closing time, but then Vincent would take his car and follow her, to first stop at an all-night coffee shop slightly north near Church Avenue for a bite to eat. Finishing up, they would go to her apartment and spend the night together.

They never really got past knowing each other much beyond these physical encounters. Whatever were her reasons for picking him up, it remained at just that level, a pick-up. Vincent didn't mind. He wasn't really looking for that much of a commitment with someone. He was young, and independent.

He was only twenty-one years old and somewhat restless, with the presence of the draft, and general uncertainty contributing to the mix in this relationship. He wasn't thinking about any kind of long-term involvement or being in love with a woman, not even Jane.

And then, as he thought it might end, Jane drove into the station one night, but she wasn't there for a fill-up. She told him that she was moving away. That could have been true, or not. She wouldn't be taking him home anymore.

"Listen, Vincent, this was really nice while it lasted, but I have to go," she said, as she sat in her car with the engine running.

"That's too bad, Jane," he answered. "Sorry we couldn't keep this going," as he leaned in her window. "You are really great, and I liked being with you."

"You're adorable," she said. "Hope things work out for you," with sincerity. She smiled at him. "Take it easy, honey." She put the car in gear, and drove onto the avenue.

He walked slowly back to his chair. He was disappointed, but not too upset.

It had been a busy few months but there wasn't much there in the way of deep feelings on the part of either one of them. It had been handy and anonymous. He would miss the convenient sex, which was good, but like Jane, even he knew that changes needed to be made.

Vincent stayed at the gas station through the fall, but as the winter approached, he made the decision to leave school where he wasn't accomplishing much in the way of pursuing a serious education, and he didn't want to be outdoors in the cold weather pumping gas. He had to face the next phase of his life.

Sure enough, once he didn't register for school, about a month later he received his 1-A draft re-classification in the mail. He didn't wait until he received the draft notice. Without much hesitation, he went to the local Navy recruiting station, and was able to complete his enlistment application within two weeks.

He was informed that one of the jobs he could train for could be as an Engineman, a mechanic for small boat motors. Perfect. Following his induction at Fort Hamilton on the southern edge of Brooklyn, he would be starting Boot Camp a few weeks later, in Great Lakes, Illinois just outside of Chicago, and Milwaukee. His father, mother and siblings, along with the rest of his family, were concerned, but supported his decision which seemed to make sense to them – probably avoiding the worst of the fighting.

He gave his notice to Frank at the gas station, and parted company with his pals, Slim Willy and Big Bill. They wished him well, telling him to take care of himself out there. He said his goodbyes to his family and friends, and he would sell his car to a guy in the neighborhood for $350.

But the last ride that he took one night in that big Chevy was along the full length of gasoline alley, slowly passing every station, to have one final look for a fast, hot blue Mustang being handled expertly by the car's perfectly matched driver.

Taxicab Rides

Douglas Miller was a taxicab driver working in Brooklyn, and everywhere else in New York City. He spent lots of hours cruising through the streets, with some adventures, and always with the threat of danger. At that time in the late 1960s drivers were paid a 55 % - 45 % split of whatever fares they booked, with the cabby getting the short end. It paid pretty well though, depending on how busy one hustled on the shift, along with how good or bad the weather was, at what time of which day or night it was, and where in the city one was willing to pick-up, and deliver passengers.

In those days if a driver worked hard, one could net an average of about $250 a week steady, which was pretty good money then, equating to about three times that amount in today's dollars.

Douglas did have to book adequate fares during every twelve-hour shift from 3:00 p.m. to about 3:00 a.m. six days a week, in order to stay employed. That is, to satisfy his bosses he had to transport enough passengers who paid enough money to cover the fleet owner's overhead.

Driving a cab was somewhat of an entrepreneurial enterprise even though he was working for the company.

He was basically on his own, to determine for himself where in the city he would work, at least until a fare took him to somewhere that he hadn't planned on, or if there were other distractions.

Even in those days when the war in Vietnam had been grinding on for years, driving a cab didn't require revealing one's draft status, to be assessed by the cab fleet owners when drivers were hired. Most other career venues did require that evaluation by employers of prospective employees.

A 1-A classification, ready for imminent induction if called, could stop the hiring process immediately at many companies. Employers were not too keen on giving candidates a chance to work, then training them, with the possibility of them leaving soon to be inducted into the Army.

To secure work as a taxicab driver was not more difficult than the process of a driver paying the additional fee to secure a Chauffeur's License, then passing the New York City Police Department background check, passing the written test, and attending the short training session. This was about all it took to secure a hack license.

Having the license, drivers could walk into a taxi garage, and if they were warm bodies breathing regularly, and were not actually on their way to jail that day, then the garage would let them have one of their fleet cabs, straight from dusk to dawn, if the drivers wanted to, with meal times on their own.

If a driver was killed during his or her shift (there were a few female drivers, but not many), which was happening to taxicab and livery drivers in those days, and continues to happen in these days, the dispatcher would have no trouble finding someone else to take that cab out for the next shift. The money was out there on the street for those willing to risk getting it.

For Douglas, who had been graduated from high school, then had kicked around the neighborhood for two years working at various part-time jobs, he needed to do something else to make more money. He had decided that he could drive a cab – there was definitely money in it.

Since his mother had died while Douglas was still in high school, he hadn't been motivated to go on to college. His father worked as a truck mechanic and didn't seem to have the expectation that Douglas would go on to college - maybe that he would attend a trade school. Douglas was not opposed to that route – he had done marginally well in school and knew that he could probably handle learning a trade, but not in a field that required hard physical labor.

Some friends of his had found jobs after high school, with some of them going on to college, securing the coveted 2-S draft deferment accorded to those students in school – a decidedly elitist status. Although somewhat concerned about being drafted into the Army to serve in Vietnam, he hadn't been overly anxious. It was something that young men did in this country – serve in the armed forces.

He didn't have any political opinion about the war – he didn't understand it much, as many other people didn't. He was watching the war on television, but he wasn't focused on it.

For the hacking life, however, the subject of the draft never came up when he interviewed for the job. After his hack license had been issued, Douglas went to one of the several taxi garages near his neighborhood. He entered the garage through the cavernous open door, past a few parked cabs, and walked up to the dispatcher's window.

"Excuse me, I just got my hack license and want to see about getting hired," he said to the older man at the window in the dispatcher's box, about at the height of the top of Douglas's shoulders. Douglas stood a thin 5'-8" tall with short brown hair, had a moderately bushy mustache and a short goatee, with friendly, but serious green eyes. He was not very imposing in stature, but presented himself with a quiet, reserved competency that others respected.

"Let me see your license," the dispatcher said flatly.

Douglas handed him his hack license.

"Let me see your driver's license," the dispatcher said, also without emotion. He looked them over.

"Okay," he said, "Fill out this application over there at one of those tables. Then bring it back to me."

"Thanks," Douglas said. He took the application and walked to one of the tables. No one else was in the garage. He had his own pen and began filling out the application. When he was finished he gave the paperwork back to the dispatcher.

He looked at it briefly, and then said, "Okay, have a seat; we'll call you in a minute."

He didn't think much about the dispatcher – looking at his licenses, and taking his application didn't require much effort. He didn't have to show any emotion, nor did he have to be civil, but it wasn't Douglas' way. About ten minutes later, the dispatcher called him over.

"The boss will see you now. Go through the door behind me on the right," he said.

"Thanks," Douglas said, and walked into the office. A large man with a cigarette in his mouth was sitting behind a very large desk.

He removed the cigarette. "Sit down," he said to Douglas, not as unfriendly as the dispatcher, but just as flat. Douglas sat in the chair next to his desk.

"My name's Freddie. I run this fleet. You're Douglas, yes? You ever drive a cab before?" he asked him.

"No sir, but I'm a good driver. My dad's a truck driver and he taught me how to drive."

"What kind of work have you done?" Freddie asked.

"I've been working since I was pretty young, and right now I'm working in my neighborhood at a couple of stores, and for a contractor. You can see from my application I've been working steady for a few years."

"Well, that's not a bad background. Since they gave you a hack license, it looks like you were never convicted of a felony. That's right, isn't it?"

"Yes, that's right. Never had any trouble with the law," he said.

"We need people who can book good money. The notes are heavy on these cabs and we need to make money. Can you make money for us?" Freddie asked him.

"I'm okay with working lots of hours, and driving all over. I could make money for you, and for myself," Douglas said.

"Don't you have a girlfriend? How old are you?" Freddie asked him.

"I do have a girlfriend, but she works a lot, too. We date off and on. She's okay with me hacking, and she wants me to make money. We'll be okay. My dad is okay with this, too, since my mom died a few years ago. And I'm twenty-one years old, anyway," Douglas said.

In those days, employers could ask lots of questions that they don't ask these days. Freddie asked, "How about getting around the city, can you find your way around?"

"I've lived in the city all my life. I know Brooklyn, Queens, the Bronx, and Manhattan," Douglas answered. "If I don't know where someplace is, I can figure it out real quick, and I'll get there. I don't know Staten Island much, but if I have to go there I'll figure it out."

Freddie looked over Douglas' paperwork again, then he said, "Alright, Douglas, I'll hire you. When can you start?"

"Let me tell my other jobs that I'm leaving. Today is Thursday. I can start next Monday," he said.

"Okay, instead of that, come in next Wednesday at three o'clock in the afternoon, and I'll have a cab for you. You can work Wednesdays through Mondays, with Tuesdays off, then back in on Wednesday through the weekend again. After the first full week I'll see what you book." Freddie handed Douglas his hack license, and driver's license.

Douglas had already thought about the hours he was going to work, and didn't hesitate. "That's fine, that will give me a chance to make more money," he said.

Freddie said, "Go out and see Bob, the dispatcher, he'll give you the W-4 form for taxes and anything else you need so you can get started, then see him next week."

Douglas stood up and extended his hand to Freddie. "Thanks, I appreciate this."

"Sounds good, kid. I'll see you next week."

Douglas went up to the dispatcher's window. "Bob?" he asked, "Freddie says to have me fill out a W-4. I'm going to start next Wednesday for a six-night shift."

Bob reached to the side of the counter behind the window, and handed Douglas the form. "Fill this out, give it back to me and I'll see you next week." Not much more acknowledgement than before.

Well, Douglas thought, he's just a face in a cage, he doesn't need much of a personality. Douglas walked out of the garage, and took the bus back to his neighborhood.

He saw his girlfriend Christine that Friday night. They had been dating for only a few months. She worked in a clothing store in the neighborhood, and similar to Douglas, had been graduated from high school three years before.

Tonight they went out to a movie. "So," Christine said to Douglas, "I guess you'll be pretty busy now."

"You know it, honey," he said. "But we'll make out. I'll be getting lots of money."

"That'll be nice," she said. "I hope I'll see you once in a while."

"Don't worry," he answered. "This can't miss. Better than me walking around the neighborhood delivering clothes or watching the suds go round and round for that gig at the Laundromat. This is a career. Maybe I'll own the company one of these days."

"I guess," Christine said. "We'll see what happens. Maybe you'll meet some girl fare and you'll dump me."

"Not a chance," he said. I'm with you for the long haul."

"Yeah, maybe," she said. "It can get intense out there, though. I've heard it can be bad, and the papers are full of drivers getting robbed and killed. You got to stay safe. I wouldn't want anything to happen to you, and I don't want to think about it." She paused. "Let's watch the movie."

Douglas hadn't thought about taxi safety or meeting someone else. He knew it was dangerous, but what could he do? He hadn't thought much about being a target, but that could happen.

He needed to make this work. For the time being he was doing alright with Christine. She was nice-looking, and fun to be with. He would see where that went.

It was 2:45 p.m. on Wednesday of the next week. He walked into the garage carrying an air-through comfort seat made of wire and plastic. He thought that this would help to keep him cool while driving in the heat of this summer. He had a clipboard for his trip sheet, to account for the number of passengers picked up per ride, and to record the fare amount collected that would have to match the meter amount, without noting any tips.

He said to the dispatcher, "Bob, my name's Douglas, you remember me from last week?"

"Yeah," Bob answered. He pulled a key from the wall, and a blank trip sheet from the counter. "Here you go, take number 221, it's over in the corner there. If it needs gas, go fill it up from the pump in the rear yard. If you need gas later, find a gas station, get a receipt, and we'll pay you back. Bring the cab back any time before about three o'clock this morning so we can give it for the next day's shift."

"Sure," Douglas answered. "Thanks." He walked over to the hack. It was a dented, beat-up, three-year old yellow Dodge Fury. It had a big eight-cylinder engine, no air conditioning.

He placed his air seat on the driver's side, and his clipboard in the middle of the front seat, and climbed in. He started the engine and checked the gas. The tank was full, so he could just drive out.

He placed his hack license in the plastic holder on the passenger side of the dashboard, adjusted his mirrors, and eased himself out of the garage into the street, jockeying through with the rest of the drivers coming off, and onto their shifts.

He headed up a half block to 13th Avenue, a bus route. Cruising for fares, he was hoping to pick up someone quickly to get the money rolling. And there it was, a guy hailed him. He pulled over to the curb and the fare climbed into the back seat.

"I can't wait for the bus," he said. "Get me to 39th and 11th Avenue."

"Sure," Douglas said. This was a short, ten-minute ride down this avenue, and then over two more. Douglas pushed the start button on the meter, and it began clicking money, for waiting time, and for mileage.

The days of the metal flag device on the meter that a driver would pull down to start the clock and the mileage calculator had recently been replaced with a more modern button starter in all cab fleets throughout the city.

Besides that a driver could actively start the meter, the seats in all cabs were "hot." They had been wired with pressure devices to sense when passengers sat down, which would start the meters automatically within about fifteen seconds after a fare climbed in.

This would prevent cabbies from "arming" the ride. That is, from striking a deal with a passenger for a set price for the trip, then being able to keep all of the fare by not having the meter record it, nor the driver recording the fare on the trip sheet.

If a driver worked at it, he or she could figure out how to disengage the sensing device, and could "arm" selected rides for a portion of the shift.

Drivers would still have to legitimately book enough on their shift to show that they were working and making money for the garage, but it could get lucrative making book on the side.

Douglas wasn't there yet mentally for the cheating side of hacking; he had just started working. He would never take that route anyway while he was a cabbie. It just wasn't in his nature. As he found out while he worked for the next year and a half, he would be making enough money in bookings, and tips to stay honest.

Douglas drove the passenger to his location, collected the $1.75 fare and received a $ .25 cent tip. Not bad, Douglas thought. He turned north and went back to the main avenue, hoping for another pick-up. He was going to make his way toward busy Manhattan if he could, where the real money was.

He was picturing the money in spite of the risks and wasn't thinking about the discomfort of driving hour after hour in the midst of traffic in the heat of the summer, without air conditioning.

Some of these vehicles, although only a few years old, had close to 100,000 miles on the odometer – this one had 82,000 miles on it.

Douglas would find out during the next winter that the cabs did have heat, but he would be driving in all kinds of weather – people needed cabs all year round, regardless if it was hot, cold, or wet outside.

During a particular shift a driver would just have to find out if he or she would be robbed of all that had been earned that day. They would also find out if they would continue to live on that day, or if on that day they would be killed.

Douglas looked down at the lockable safe mounted on the transmission hump that he could put his money in, however, he would always need to keep money available on his person to make change, and the key to unlock the box was back at the garage.

If he would use the safe, which he would subsequently never do, then in order to get his money to turn in to the dispatcher at the end of the shift, he would need to have the dispatcher unlock it, which took time. Douglas would not use the safe but would keep the money handy and would turn in what he booked, with the rest unaccounted for until tax time. He would find out that other drivers didn't use these safes either.

Almost all of them kept their money in various pants and shirt pockets. The bad guys also knew this.

Some of these people riding cabs for profit would kill you for any amount of money that a driver was carrying, regardless if the bulk of it would have been kept in the safe, so what difference did it make how much or how little a driver had, or where they carried it?

He continued along 13th Avenue towards Coney Island Avenue, another major bus route that would lead to the expressway into Manhattan, hoping to catch a fare on his way there.

He took the pencil that he used to record the trip sheet out of his top shirt pocket, and jabbed it into one of the existing pencil holes that had been stabbed into a corner of the dashboard.

He could see that pencils were not always placed into the same hole, since other drivers used the same cab, and the dashboard was pretty well poked up.

He caught another rider along the avenue; an older man holding a suitcase was standing there in front of a house. This had possibilities.

"I'm going to Kennedy. I need to catch a Pan Am flight, and I need to get there fast," he said.

"Yes sir," Douglas said. He noted the current time, also that this trip was with one passenger, and where he picked him up. He punched the meter and took off, turning at the next corner to head south to the airport.

This was a golden moment. This would be about a twenty-dollar ride – a big fare. Catching this in the middle of Brooklyn, not bad, he thought.

There was some conversation, not much, mostly about the weather, traffic, and some sports.

Douglas would find that some passengers were very talkative, and some were absolutely non-communicative. If they talked, fine, but then Douglas was sometimes the entertainment, and sometimes the passengers were very animated. If they didn't talk much, then Douglas could just drive.

They arrived at the airport terminal about a half-hour later. Douglas collected his fare, plus a one-dollar tip and discharged his passenger.

He noted where he had dropped him off, then made his way over to the cab stand near the arriving international flights, hoping to catch a ride into Manhattan.

It didn't take long. A flight had recently arrived and there were enough fares stepping into the cabs that were waiting. Douglas caught two people heading into mid-town Manhattan – another twenty-dollar ride. He was doing really well for his first day on the job.

Once he had delivered his passengers to their hotel, Douglas pulled into traffic to cruise along a main avenue. He picked up fare after fare for the rest of the afternoon and evening, and well into the morning.

He finally called it a night about 2:00 a.m., and headed back into Brooklyn. He rode empty, which was not the best scenario, however, it wasn't always easy to get a fare going to one of the outer boroughs at that hour, and he had to bring the cab in. It had been a great first shift.

He arrived at the garage, and pulled into a spot. Other cabs were coming in as well. He collected his things, walked over to the dispatch window where the night man was counting bills, and turned in his money and trip sheet.

He had booked seventy-eight dollars that day. It was a great haul for a Wednesday. He expected that he would be booking lots more on the weekends.

And he was going to get just a shade under half of that and everything else that he booked for each shift on payday. The days of cabbies taking their cut in cash on the same shift that they turned in their bookings were over

Their share was now calculated by the garage afterwards, and turned into a weekly payroll check. Douglas did not turn in his tip money which totaled about seven dollars.

He left the garage and walked to the bus stop. It was 3:30 a.m. He waited about forty minutes for the bus. He was tired, but elated. And he would be doing the same thing the next day.

For the rest of that week, over the weekend, and into the next week, he drove long hours, picked up and delivered many passengers, had superficial and philosophic conversations with many strangers, and booked a good deal of money. He had eaten lots of different sandwiches and pizza slices, using restrooms wherever he could.

On Wednesday of the next week, as Douglas picked up his first paycheck, and was handed the keys for a cab, Bob said, "Douglas, go in and see Freddie before you head out."

"Sure," Douglas answered. He opened his envelope and saw from the check stub that he had grossed two-hundred and seventy nine dollars after the split of his bookings, netting two-hundred and twenty-five dollars. With his tips for the week coming to more than forty dollars, he was in the money.

He walked to the office, knocked on the door, and Freddie asked him to come in. "Douglas, you made good money this first week. So far so good, kid. Keep it up and you should have no problem to keep working here," Freddie told him.

"Thanks, Freddie, glad you're okay with this. I felt like I had a good week, and I'll keep it up. Thanks."

Douglas left the office, and got into the cab that he had been assigned to by Bob. It was another clunker, with a loose front end, but it had a full tank of gas. He left the garage, and headed onto the main avenue, as he had been doing for the past week. He wondered how much money he would make tonight, and if anything would happen to him to interfere with that.

The cabs had sliding plastic partitions installed between the front and rear seats to protect the driver, but they were not bullet-proof. The framing didn't fit completely tight to the door post but left a gap, so someone could just stick a gun through there.

Even if a criminal didn't have a gun, they could push a knife through this space into the driver's neck.

And, of course, the driver did have to open the sliding partition quite a bit to take payments, and make change leaving a nice wide open space for the criminals to use any weapon of choice.

Later in the year, the garage would replace the old fleet with new cabs that had some serious, tightly sealed steel partitioning; however, the glass of car doors is not bullet-proof. All anyone had to do was to step out of the cab after paying the driver through the little metal tray in the center of the partition, then move to the driver's side of the cab, and blast the driver in the head through the window. There was nothing frivolous about the dangers of driving a cab.

He didn't think about these things for too long, though, since he picked up a fare pretty quickly after leaving the garage, a local job. From that drop-off, he was captured into driving to various places within Brooklyn, mostly short rides. He just could not seem to maneuver into Manhattan.

Some shifts were going to be that way. He didn't want to give up too early and drive empty into Manhattan, but many nights he did just that to move things along.

There were many older drivers with either fleet cabs or their own cabs who were cruising Brooklyn streets, and were waiting at various cab stands, but the serious money was generally in Manhattan.

His next few weeks were basically uneventful. He went out with Christine whenever he could, and just kept on doing what he was doing.

Sometimes he even had some cheap thrills. One early evening at rush hour, he was waiting at a particular taxi stand next to an elevated subway station. There was a women's clothing store along the block near the street corner. The dressing room was located next to a display window, thinly shielded by a slightly parted curtain. What were they thinking of at this store?

As he waited at this stand, creeping slowly forward as each cab in front of him was taken by the next passenger or group leaving the train station, he was angled just right to actually watch a customer taking off her clothes to try on an outfit. The woman had no idea that she could be seen – and on more than one occasion, every once in a while at this stand, Douglas saw plenty. Really cheap thrills, indeed.

It wasn't all fun and games, though. One late afternoon he was waiting at a cab stand near another subway station on 5th Avenue, in the neighborhood of Bay Ridge.

He was hoping to pick up some quick local jobs from commuters returning from work, before he could launch his way into Manhattan for the busy evening.

A woman walked up to his cab, jumped in, and said, "Please, you need to go around the corner to get my daughter – we need to get her to the hospital, right now. I think she's having an appendicitis attack. We have to hurry."

Douglas didn't say a word, not even to think to ask why she wasn't calling an ambulance, but maybe that would have cost more money than a cab ride, or the ambulance never showed up. He punched the meter and took off.

They arrived at her house on the next block. Douglas jumped out with the mother, and walked up the steps to help the daughter into the front seat.

The mother was now joined by the father who got into the back seat of the cab. The daughter was doubled over and holding her stomach.

The father said, "I know she's having an appendicitis attack. We called for an ambulance, but it never came, and I knew that we had to get going, so I sent my wife around the corner for a cab."

"Good thing I was there," Douglas said. "Don't worry everyone, we'll get there right away."

He put on the headlights, and the four-way emergency flashers, and raced through the traffic east on 4th Avenue, to the nearest hospital, about a mile away, honking his horn through every intersection.

He was trying as much as possible not to bounce the cab. The daughter was just holding her middle, groaning steadily.

He was approaching the hospital from the wrong street to be able to turn directly to the emergency room entrance, and needed to be on the next north avenue.

He didn't think that he had enough time to do that, so he drove into the one way street the wrong way.

This was a much faster means to get to the emergency room entrance than going completely around the block. He took his chances on hitting any on-coming cars. He stopped the cab at the entrance. The hospital team had been alerted that they were coming.

Several hospital personnel ran into the street, and took the daughter out of the cab. The father gave Douglas his fare, and a nice tip. Exciting, but just routine, Douglas thought humbly.

Calls went from medical emergencies to cultural urgencies, however. One night Douglas was cruising in lower Manhattan, near Greenwich Village. Two women hailed him. They climbed in and one of them said, "Hi, taxicab man, we're on our way to a party. I think it's on 12th Street near 8th Avenue, maybe about in the middle of the block."

Although her speech was a little slurred, both of them were dressed neatly, and looked very nice. They seemed to be coming from another party when they had hailed his cab. Douglas drove them around for a few blocks, getting acquainted.

They weren't completely clear on the exact address of where this next party was taking place, but no matter, the three of them were having a great time, and they had introduced themselves as Betty, and Connie. As they had told Douglas, they were twenty-eight, and twenty-five, respectively.

Finally, it was getting to be too much of an effort for them to locate the place, and Douglas was getting really friendly with Connie, in spite of thinking about Christine in the back of his mind. After all, he and Christine weren't married, they were just dating.

Then, after driving for about twenty minutes, now near Broadway and 16th Street, Betty said, "You know what, I want to get dropped off here, I need to see somebody."

"You're bailing on me?" said Connie.

"Yeah," she said. "I'm going to skip the party. But you, baby, looks like maybe you can still ride with Douglas."

"You know it," she said. "I'm liking this."

Douglas said, "You're okay here on this corner?"

"Really, Doug, I'm good. I'll be fine, I just need to see this guy about something." She was speaking a little sloppily, but not too badly.

Douglas stopped the cab and she got out. "So long," she said. "And you Doug, you take it easy, been good to know you."

"Sure, it's been a slice."

Once she left, Douglas said, "Any idea where we're headed?"

"I don't live too far from here," she answered. "How about we go back to my place?"

"That works for me," Douglas said. "Just point me in the right direction."

"I'm over on East 4th Street, near 2nd Avenue."

"Fine, I'll find a place to park over there," Douglas said.

He drove the few blocks to that part of the neighborhood, and parked on a side street. Exiting the cab, and walking to her apartment, he didn't leave the meter running.

Yes, it was somewhat despicable to engage in this sort of pleasure, with him being in a relationship with his current girlfriend, but he was young, and had flexible morals. Lots of young people had adaptable morality in those days.

He stayed with Connie for a few hours, and then he needed to get back to work. As casually as this had started earlier that evening, so it ended the same way.

Douglas left the apartment, and didn't collect his fare – he would just add that amount to the book from his own money.

This kind of thing was pretty unusual. He never went back to see this woman, never even thought to get her telephone number. It had simply been a warm, friendly interlude, just a spur of the moment sharing, a cabdriver's dream.

About the closest to that happening again to Douglas was one night a few months later, when a young woman hailed him on a mid-town Manhattan street, and needed to go about ten miles north through the city way up to the Bronx.

She told him right up front that she didn't have the full fare, but that she really had no other way of getting there. Douglas thought about suggesting an alternate payment plan, but he could tell that she didn't appear to be that willing for such an arrangement, and Douglas was generally a nice guy.

"Well, I really need to make this a paying proposition," Douglas said to her. "It's about a five-dollar ride. How much do you have?"

She opened her handbag. "I've only got four dollars," she said.

"Anything else?" Douglas asked.

"Well, I have an apple and an orange in this other bag," she said.

"Tell you what," he said to her, "Let's settle for two of those dollars, and the apple. I can live with that."

"Wow," she said, "That is really great, thank you so much."

"It's okay, sometimes that's how it has to be," he said philosophically. The rest of the ride was uneventful. He brought her to the Bronx, dropped her off, and ate the apple.

There were other vignettes. For example, something as simple, and fun as Douglas marking down on his trip sheet that he had carried two passengers instead of one when a pregnant woman got in – that was kind of cute.

Another time, with the new fleet cabs, a device that these cabs had were big, bulbous, water-filled, black rubber bumpers both front and back.

They were someone's idea of how to protect the cars, and occupants from crashes. They must have added a lot of weight to the cab with all of that water, maybe twenty gallons, but they really worked, as Douglas had the opportunity to test this contraption one night.

He was alone in the cab, driving down a busy street looking for a fare when, for whatever reason, the car in front of him just stopped, a typical New York City driving maneuver. They weren't going that fast or it might have been more serious.

Douglas stopped short, but not short enough. He hit the stopped car in front of him and whoomp! A huge splash of water spurted out from the popped plugs at the top of the bumper.

Douglas jumped out of the cab and there was water everywhere, but there was no damage to either of the cars.

What a concept. This technology didn't last too long as these devices were kind of ugly, and heavy, but they did do a great job for this kind of minor accident.

Since the driver in front had caused the accident, and there was no damage to either vehicle, they didn't even bother to exchange driver's licenses, or insurance information, if the driver of the stopped car even had insurance. This was fine with Douglas. He wouldn't even need to report the accident.

Later that night he pulled into a gas station and used their water hose to re-fill the bumper, pushing the plugs back in. Nothing else came of the encounter.

But there was also drama. On one shift, about mid-night, a guy hailed the cab and had Douglas take him to several different local bars where he went in, stayed awhile, and then came out for Douglas to drive him to another bar.

The meter was ticking away. This didn't look good to Douglas. At about the fourth place that Douglas had taken him, Douglas was waiting, and waiting, and waiting. It was now about 1:30 a.m.

Douglas got tired of waiting, and went in after him – he wasn't there! The bartender said that this guy was in here a minute ago, and had just left out the back door.

Douglas ran out of the bar and hopped back into the cab, swung it around the corner, onto the next block – and there he was.

Douglas jumped the cab right over the curb, stopping just short from crushing the guy against a building – after all, Douglas was a professional driver; he knew how to do this.

Douglas leaped out while the guy was still frozen against the wall in a drunken shock. Douglas was not a big guy, but when he needed to be ferocious, he could make it real.

"Put your wallet on the hood, you meatball," Douglas hissed at him.

The guy squeezed his hand into his back pocket and placed his wallet on the hood. He knew that he had been defeated, but was still alive.

Douglas took out what the guy owed him on the meter, about eight dollars, and grabbed another two dollars as a generous tip for his aggravation.

After all, if this guy could buy drinks for the past hour or so, he could pay Douglas, with tip. He placed the wallet back on the hood.

"Take it, man, and don't you ever do that to any other cabbie again, you hear me?" Douglas was angry, but steady.

"I got it, buddy," he said. He didn't stick around. Douglas got back in his cab, and backed out onto the street. It was time to call it a night and return to the garage. Besides the appendicitis rescue, and his romantic rendezvous, this was probably the most exciting episode that Douglas had ever had while hacking. Just another day on the night shift.

Although there was the time that Douglas raced a gypsy cab at seventy miles per hour for about a mile southbound on the West Side Highway.

A gypsy is a livery cab without a medallion, which is the franchise-like metal permit affixed to the hood authorizing an operator to pick-up fares on the street.

The West Side Highway, a major artery in Manhattan that hugs the Hudson River, was still paved with cobble-stones in the late 1960s. As Douglas and the livery driver swerved at street level through the massive steel stanchions supporting the upper roadway, it was quite a contest – who says you can't make seventy miles per hour in a thirty mile per hour zone?

Douglas figured that he won, but the other driver just took off after they were finished. No matter, at least there were no crashes.

And the time that the motor mounts let go on one of the old cabs that Douglas was driving, while in traffic on a busy, hot, sweltering summer night. This sent the entire engine flopping over on its side. This was not fun to Douglas.

He managed to pull over to the curb in all of that traffic, and shut the engine off. Douglas left the cab and saw a pay phone in front of a store.

"Hey, Joey," he said to the dispatcher on duty. "I've got cab # 307 and the motor mounts just broke – the engine is on its side. I can't drive this thing, and I need a tow or another cab. I'm on 85th Street off of 6th Avenue in Brooklyn."

"Okay, man, we'll get out to you as soon as we can, just stay there," Joey said.

"Sure, Joey, I'm not going anywhere," Douglas answered.

Douglas waited, sitting on the cab, since it was way too hot to sit in it. After an hour, a dented, unmarked car pulled up next to him. It was Anthony, one of the mechanics from the garage.

"How you doing, man?" Anthony asked. "What happened?"

"Hey, Anthony," Douglas said. "Good to see you. I'm just driving down the street when the engine falls over, revving up to twenty million RPMs."

"Yeah, that's rough, but I'll get you out of here."

"Great, let's get going, I've got money to make."

"Douglas, here's what we're going to do. I'm going to push you back to the garage," Anthony told him.

"You're going to push me five miles through this traffic to the garage?" Douglas said. "What about a tow truck?" Douglas asked.

"No man, no tow truck, no wrecker," Anthony said. "Don't worry, we'll make it."

Douglas was not too happy – it took skill, and nerves to be pushed, and the same for someone to do the pushing, but if that's all the garage was going to offer, then this is what needed to happen.

Anthony and Douglas pushed the cab away from the curb, and angled it as straight as possible. Anthony maneuvered his car behind it.

Douglas got in to his cab, and turned the key to accessories, so that he would have lights; then he placed the shifter into neutral.

"Ready, let's go," Douglas shouted back to Anthony, while waving his arm forward. This was going to be a long ride.

After about an hour, they did make their way back to the garage, without causing any accidents or killing anyone. Douglas was glad it was over.

"Thanks, Anthony," Douglas said as he was shaking his hand. "You got me back in one piece – nice going!"

"Anytime my friend," Anthony said. "I'm glad I'm back, too."

"Yeah, you and me both," Douglas laughed.

Douglas had lost more than two hours so far, but it was still early enough to go back out there. He walked up to Joey the dispatcher. Bob was off this night.

"Joey, I need another cab," he said.

"Okay, I can let you have # 18," Joey said. "Good car, even has a radio. The guy that put the radio in it is off tonight. Try not to lose the motor in this one; the guy really likes # 18."

"Don't worry. I'm just going to see if I can lose the wheels," Douglas quipped.

"Yeah, sure, well, anyway, I'll see you later," Joey said as he handed him the key.

Douglas spent another four hours out there that night after the disintegration of his first car, but he was glad to be back on the streets.

Several more months passed. He went through the winter, when sometimes the weather was extremely arduous to drive through, but he worked on anyway – this is what he did.

He went through the spring, which was usually an easier season to drive in, barring rain. He was glad to be making money, and was also meeting many people while hacking. Some of them were regular individuals, some were really weird.

Douglas was a union member, had an air seat that he carried from cab to cab, and had a clipboard - he was living a ubiquitous sub-cultural existence. Unfortunately, he and Christine had broken up. They just didn't seem to have enough time to be with each other. It was only one of several relationships that Douglas would have in his lifetime.

Once the next summer came around, a sense of isolation was beginning to creep in, as he was deep within the entrails of the beast on the filthy, degenerative streets.

He would have meals of hot and cold hero sandwiches, sitting on park benches or in his cab. He would find toilet facilities wherever he could, in commercial establishments, gas stations or standing behind the open door of his cab.

He gathered with the other cabbies in the garage on many late afternoons waiting for the shift to change. He exchanged selected stories, sometimes of boredom, though sometimes with relish. These activities dispelled any folklore that he might have believed was attached to being a taxicab driver.

He hadn't yet been affected enough by the atmosphere out there that would cause him to reach the deep level of psychological isolation, and mental fatigue that one could fall into by driving a cab. Hacking could have the electrifying attraction of being a part of storied popular culture as depicted in many stories and movies; however, one could miss realizing beforehand its capability to breed a terrifying loneliness.

Douglas' identification, and empathy was the recognition that he shared the sensation of suffocating within humanity while being emotionally separated from other people. These thoughts came to him way before the devastating film that would be produced in 1976 by Martin Scorsese, starring Robert DeNiro, et al., in "Taxi Driver," a depiction of acute psychosis, and the underworld of hacking.

Douglas did have close family ties, and other relationships, so the trauma of cruising alone in the streets in the midst of civilization did not have the same negative affect on him as it did for Travis Bickle, the main character in this film. Douglas was living this hacking life, though, way far in from the edge.

It would be while Douglas was still on the job, though, when Harry Chapin's song, "Taxi," was released, where he describes picking up a fare one night, a woman from his long-ago past.

They each reminisce about loss, missed opportunities, choices. It was spooky for Douglas listening to this song, a real vision for him.

When the lyrics described the driver placing the large $20.00 tip that he received from his lost love in his shirt, Douglas felt his spine tingle – it's just what he and other drivers usually did with money that they weren't going to use again that night.

Douglas never did meet a long-lost someone while driving, but he could see that it might come to that in the future if he kept this up – that is, if he wasn't stopped by external forces.

He knew it was time for a change, but he just didn't know which direction he wanted to go. The draft was still a factor, although now enforced by a lottery drawing, however, he had a very low number, and could be drafted anytime. He didn't think that he would necessarily be shipped off to Vietnam in these later days of the war, but it could happen.

In any case, his life would be interrupted by the military in a major way – interrupted from being a wandering generality cruising through the streets, waiting for fortune or tragedy, to possibly becoming a statistic, or a footnote in political history.

One early evening, he stopped at a cabstand at a quiet subway station in Bay Ridge, a neighborhood at the western edge of Brooklyn.

He had pulled in behind a large Checker cab, which was the classic vehicle with two extra "jump seats" in the rear passenger section – a taxi limousine compared to the standard sedans that most fleets were running.

Douglas left his cab to join the other driver who was leaning on the side of his Checker. "Hey, how you doing?" Douglas said to him.

"I'm alright, buddy, how about yourself?" he asked. He seemed to be a little older than Douglas, but not by much.

"You know how it is, slow night, hot, what else is new?" Douglas said. "Where's your garage?" Douglas asked.

"I'm way over in East New York," he said. "I was heading to the airport when I caught a guy that wanted me to take him around here on the other side of Brooklyn."

"Yeah, I know how that goes," Douglas said. "Happens all the time. You think you're going somewhere that you want to go, then, you're not."

"I know what you mean," the driver said. "Where's your fleet?" He asked.

"Me? I'm in Borough Park, but I go anywhere, wherever the money is," Douglas said.

"Yeah, I know that route. How long you been doing this?" he asked.

"A little more than a year." Douglas answered. "It's a grind, but I'm making money."

"Yeah, me too," said the driver. "My name's Gregory, what's yours?" he asked.

"I'm Douglas," he answered.

"I just started doing this a few months ago when I got out of the Air Force," Gregory said.

"How long were you in? Where were you stationed?" Douglas asked him.

"Oh, I was at Yokota Air Base near Tokyo in Japan. I was in for three years," he said.

"What were you doing there?" Douglas asked.

"I was a hydraulics mechanic, an E-4 Corporal," he said.

"How did you like it?" asked Douglas.

"It was work, some military stuff, but it was great being overseas," he answered. "When I got out I had two really expensive cameras, and a stereo system that I got cheap over there. I had a car that I sold before I was separated from active duty, and two-thousand dollars cash money in my pocket that I saved up. I was high on the hog, man. I'm just driving a hack now until I see what I want to do. Maybe go to school under the GI Bill."

"That's great," Douglas said. "What made you go into the Air Force?"

"Well, the Army draft was really coming close, and I couldn't see myself on the ground in Vietnam, not that noise for me, so I joined up with the Air Force, since I was working as a mechanic after I got out of high school."

"Sounds good, Gregory," Douglas said. "I've been thinking about the service myself, since I have a really low draft number. I don't know that I would have to go to 'Nam, but we're still watching that stuff on TV and it's no place that I want to be."

"I lost a friend of mine over there," Gregory said. "It was bad. I didn't want that to happen to me, no matter that I'm a righteous American."

"I know how you feel," Douglas said. "I grew up in Cub Scouts, and all of that, said my Pledge of Allegiance and Psalm 23 all the years in school, but I don't know that I'm ready to give my life for, well, I don't know what I would be giving my life for, and regardless of that we should support our country."

"Well, maybe we could support most of what this country is all about, but, you know, the war in Vietnam just seems to be taking an awful lot of lives for I don't know what either," Gregory said. "I was in the Air Force. I did my part, for what it's worth."

Douglas was impressed with what Gregory had told him. Gregory had been in other parts of the world; he had experiences, and opportunities.

He seemed to be doing alright now, and certainly was no longer concerned about the draft. Food for Douglas' thoughts, for sure.

A train rumbled into the station below. Gregory and Douglas said goodbye, and climbed into their cabs. Fares came out from the station, and they were both at work again.

Several more months went by with Douglas driving, and picking up fares, and tallying up his book, and waiting in the garage for his next cab, and sleeping into the late morning. Douglas began to be really restless.

Finally, he made a decision to take action. He went to the local Coast Guard recruiting station. He met with a Chief Petty Officer, and was able to secure a billet.

He signed up for Boot Camp, and would take his training in Cape May, New Jersey. His father, and the rest of his family were on his side for this.

One night in November, before the snows came, he turned in his bookings, and told the dispatcher, "Bob, I'm giving you two weeks notice. I'm going to move on past hacking."

"Yeah, what are you going to do?" Bob said. One of the few times Bob had ever said anything personal to Douglas, or to any other driver, for that matter.

"I signed on for the Coast Guard," he said.

"Well, good luck to you," he said. "You don't have to give me two weeks. This is a shape job. Most drivers just come and go, but that's up to you."

"That's just the way I operate," he said. "I'll finish up this shift, and next week's, then I'm clearing out."

During the next two weeks, Douglas drove his nights, collected his pay, and wasn't anxious now about what he was going to do for his future.

He was thinking about what it was going to be like in the service, but he was no longer concerned about the draft. For him, being fortunate enough to be able to join the Coast Guard was very positive.

As for driving a cab, Douglas had seen a lot, had been to a lot of places in the city, and had made a good amount of money. He had mostly put his money away, and had contributed to the household.

He never did get around to buying a car before he left for training. No matter about owning a car, he wouldn't need one now. And besides, he had taken enough car rides in taxicabs to last him for a good long while.

Class "A" School

The main barracks at the U.S. Naval Educational Training Center in Great Lakes, Illinois, some twenty-five miles south of Milwaukee, Wisconsin, was a huge building affectionately known to one and all as the "Castle." Maybe they called it the Castle because of how it was laid out with four massive corner blocks of rooms surrounding a courtyard - or maybe because of the cockroaches that marched around in there like knights of old.

It was a structure built in the late 1950s, of standard concrete block walls, configured into several four-person open cubicles on each of three floors, with vinyl composition tile flooring, pendant-hung fluorescent lighting, four individual stand-up metal lockers, two writing tables and two bunk beds, or racks, to shelter four sailors in each of these spaces.

It would be Kevin Saunder's residence for the next three months while he attended this Class "A" training school, covering the theory, and operation of shipboard high pressure propulsion steam plants. His rating was Boiler Tender (BT), also known as Boiler Technician or Water Tender, indicating the obvious responsibilities to fire up the boilers, and to monitor the water feed to make steam to drive the main engines and auxiliary equipment of Navy ships.

Boiler Tender was a term derived from the earlier titles used by the Navy and the Merchant Marine of Oiler, Wiper or Stoker, who were tasked with lubricating and maintaining machinery in the engineering spaces, and for shoveling coal into the boiler fireboxes.

Boiler operators, and stokers were also known collectively as the Black Gang, a carryover from those coal-firing days, and later applied to the use of # 6 grade black oil, or the heavier tar-like Bunker "C" oil which was heated with steam pipes running through the storage tanks to thin out its viscosity before using it to fire the boilers. One other collective name for the boiler gang was "snipe" with one legend noting that these individuals cannot stand direct sunlight or fresh air.

Kevin had been recommended for this technical training following his previous one year service on a destroyer in the fleet, operating the plant on his ship. He was an E-3 Fireman, equivalent to a Private First Class in the Army. It was the fall of 1971.

He had a suitable physique for this rating, as he was not a large man, only 5'-7" tall, but slimly muscular, which provided him with the ability to carry heavy things, and to squeeze into very small spaces within pressure vessels. With short-cropped brown hair, hazel eyes, and being clean-shaven, the soot and grime of the boilers would fit him well. His youth of twenty-one years old and good physical condition added to his capability to meet the challenges of boiler work.

When he left boot camp, he joined his assigned ship out of San Diego, California. The operating theatre had then been in the Western Pacific, and the Gulf of Tonkin, providing naval gunfire support off the coast of Vietnam. Once the ship had rotated back to San Diego he had then been TAD, ordered to Temporary Assigned Duty, at the school in Great Lakes.

After arriving at the school, although Kevin was assigned to a room in one of the Castle blocks, for a few days he had not been assigned to a watch section, and was relatively free to amuse himself on the base. He found the pool hall, and spent some time there with several other sailors whom he had met. After some days of playing, and waiting, he was assigned to a class with other technicians.

Attending classes, labs, and homework took up most of the typical weekdays. The sailors were instructed in basic thermodynamics, steam theory, steam plant operations, and the repair of boilers, pumps, fans and valves. Lab work involved testing, and analysis of water and fuel. This was science, on the brink of chemistry, at a high school level.

The equipment in the multi-million dollar fire rooms on these ships demanded the skills of people who could absorb a lot of basic information, and could think on their feet. For some sailors, their operating and repair skills were based completely on practical experience, on the job training.

For others, if selected, their abilities were enhanced by a period of formal classroom instruction, and the opportunity to operate a functioning stationary steam plant set up as if on board ship.

Some systems in the engineering spaces were complicated, some were not, but the rating of Boiler Tender required a lot more than just muscle.

It wasn't exactly easy; it wasn't exactly simple, but most anyone could learn it if one paid attention. If one weren't careful, one could be killed or hurt very badly. Almost all Navy Boiler Tenders were assigned to the fire rooms on ships against their will. There were almost no volunteers for this rating – the working conditions at constant, horrendous temperatures of 110° F to 180° F were virtually unbearable, almost beyond human endurance, but these sailors somehow persevered.

The technical training, however, would go a long way in preparing those sailors who had never been aboard ships to be better equipped for operating these propulsion plants, and would supplement the practical experience for those who had been to the fleet.

For some, this technical training, and hands-on experience during their naval careers would be of great benefit for later pursuit of civilian careers in similar fields.

At Class "A" school liberty for the sailors was just about every weeknight and weekend unless one had the duty, perhaps once a month. This watch would be as a rotating "supernumerary," that is, a non-essential thing with minimal responsibilities.

These included cleaning the head, or lavatory on each floor, or for sweeping down selected stairways. It was not very difficult. The sailors weren't even restricted to Cinderella Liberty, that is, the requirement to be back on base by midnight – they almost always had liberty privileges until 0700 the next morning.

Most of the students did not go out during the week since there was studying to be done. Also, the weather was cold during this winter, and there wasn't much happening on the commercial strip in the town of Waukegan just outside the base. The weekends were mostly quiet for many of them, busy for others.

Being busy is what happened to Kevin, and his buddy Tim Raphus, another E-3 from the fleet. One night Tim came back to the Castle from Milwaukee where he had gone to visit a cousin of his who was working in town.

Tim came into the cubicle that he shared with Aiden and Terry, who had not been to the fleet yet, and Kevin, his steaming buddy, and said, "Get this man, I was on my way to the bus station tonight and passed by a phone booth when the phone started ringing. I couldn't help it, I picked it up and said 'Hello, who's this?' A woman answered, 'Hello yourself, who's this?' I said, 'I'm Tim, who's this again?'"

"What do you mean?" Kevin interrupted, "She just started talking to you?"

"I kid you not, buds, she starts talking and then I start talking. She tells me she's in college and we talk a little more about me being in school at the base."

"Then I tell her maybe we should get together. You know, this was pretty weird, but I was just doing it. Before you know it, I'm making a date with her for myself and with a friend of hers, for you, for next weekend."

"I'm hearing you on this tale and I'm in, man, but I don't know about this really working," Kevin said.

"Don't worry," Tim said. "This is a better prospect than us just hanging around the base next weekend shooting pool, or going to the movie theatre or lifting our elbows at the Enlisted Men's Club, right?"

"Well, maybe. We still need to spend some dough on a bus ride, then on hotel rooms to stay over on Saturday to see if this is real . . ." he trailed off. Kevin was on the edge of disbelief, but agreed that he would go with Tim into town.

They left the base on the next Saturday morning, catching a bus outside of the main gate into Milwaukee. This city was almost like a small town, only much busier, having the scale of Boston or Baltimore. Arriving downtown, they booked two rooms at the Sheraton-Schroeder. Once a really fine hotel, at this time it was way past its glory days, but still showing its elegance. Lots of marble and granite, and the bathrooms even had a separate spigot to serve ice water, though it was not operational. The nightly cost for a single room in this caliber hotel was hard to believe, a mere $7.00 – well, this was 1971.

Later in their adventures while visiting Milwaukee during the following weeks, they would stay at this hotel several times, and also at the nearby Plankington.

This was one of the city's oldest, and finest establishments; however, that reputation was in the distant past. The rate here for a single room was equally reasonable at only $10.00. The place was just as elegantly faded as the Sheraton.

Tim had arranged for them to meet the women at the Milwaukee Museum of Science and Industry. This museum had installations of period streets of Old Milwaukee with several display shops, many historical artifacts, and antique machinery. Kevin was still holding on to being skeptical that their dates would show as they waited in the entrance, but unbelievably, after a short while, they did.

"Hi," one of the women said as they walked up to them. "I'm Megan." She looked at Tim. "You must be Tim, right?"

"You're right," Tim answered brightly. She was reasonably cute, of medium height and build, with dark brown hair and dark eyes, wearing a skirt and blouse. Tim was a few inches taller than she, striking in his military haircut, with black hair and brown eyes.

"Nice to meet you. This here is my buddy Kevin like I told you on the phone."

"Hey, Megan," he said to her. She looked at her friend and said, "This is Suzanne."

He looked at Suzanne. She was mildly chunky with red hair, and green eyes. She was sweetly dressed in a casual pants suit and was just shorter than Kevin.

"Hello, Suzanne, how are you doing?" He said to her. Then, kind of formally, "I'm glad you could make it today. I was looking forward to meeting you and your friend."

And he had been, tentatively as it was. The circumstances of this date were still strange to Kevin, but now actually meeting the women, Kevin began to contemplate the possibilities.

"How about we go into the museum," Tim said.

"Sure, sounds good," said Megan.

With Tim and Megan paired up, Kevin and Suzanne began talking as they entered the exhibits.

"This was a little strange how Tim caught that phone call," Kevin said.

"I know what you mean," Suzanne said. "She was calling a friend of ours and must have dialed the wrong number. When Tim picked up the phone, they just started talking. When he told her that he was in the Navy here in Great Lakes and that he had a friend, it just seemed like we should get together. It was totally unexpected."

"Yeah, a surprise for me, too," Kevin said.

"Well, Megan and I dated sailors before and we had fun with them so maybe the connection was weird, but it worked out, didn't it?"

Kevin's thoughts were moving ahead. He was hoping that he would be having some fun with Suzanne. He wasn't sure where this was going, but for now, he was along for the ride.

Kevin would think about these days in later years, as pre-dating the 1982 film, "An Officer and a Gentleman," with Richard Gere and Debra Winger.

Kevin was just a lowly enlisted man, and not an officer candidate, so when he did look back on these times with Suzanne he did know that they would have had miles to go before they could have been movie stars involved in their intense and tender relationship, against the backdrop of military and civilian complications. When he did think about it, he was confident that the two of them, along with Tim and Megan, could have been the original cast of this movie.

"Where do you go to school?" he asked her.

"Oh, we go to the University of Wisconsin near Racine, and we live in Kenosha."

"How old are you?"

"I'm twenty, and so is Megan. We went to high school together. How old are you and Tim?"

"I'm twenty-one. Tim is twenty-three. We're at the Great Lakes base for twelve weeks of boiler school, and then we'll be going back to the fleet, probably back to Vietnam. It's nice to go out on the weekend, especially with someone like you."

She smiled. Then she said seriously, "That's too bad about the war. I hope you'll be alright."

"Well, it's not that bad on a ship off the coast. Sometimes we see action, but we do have a distance factor. Only a few times so far have we been too close to the beach, and the bullets were flying, but it's nothing to what's going on in-country."

"I'm nowhere near to the horrors of that noise. Someday, it may be over."

"I hope so," she said. "We've been in this war way too long, and for what? I can't figure it out."

"Well, I can't either, but for now I'm just in it. Meanwhile, I just do my job and try and stay focused."

"That's the best way, I guess. I was looking forward to our date today, to get away from studying," she said.

"What are you taking in school?" he asked.

"I'm going to major in business. I like to work with figures and stuff. How about you, are you staying in the Navy?"

"No, I'm in for four years, and then I'm planning on getting out, maybe to go back to college. I've already done about two years in the Navy. It's all downhill from here."

"Where did you go to school?" she asked him.

"I started at Boston College but really couldn't hack it. I guess I really wasn't ready, so I went into the service. Now I'm really thinking about going back, or just thinking about making money. I'll figure it out."

As they toured the museum, Kevin could see that Tim and Megan seemed to be getting along well, talking and leaning in to each other.

Later that afternoon after finishing their tour they went to an Italian restaurant. Although Kevin and Tim, being opportunistic sailors from the fleet, invited the women to their hotel, Megan and Suzanne didn't seem ready to visit with these men so quickly.

Here they were, just meeting them, they being strangers, and sailors as well.

The evening ended with a plan to see each other again the next weekend. Kevin and Tim got their phone number at the college.

Now dating Megan and Suzanne kept them going into Milwaukee for the rest of their time at Great Lakes. They went every one of the next several weekends of the next two months, staying at the Sheraton or at the Plankington.

They would meet the women to go bowling, or to shoot pool, or to go to the movies, then dinner. Remarkably, Suzanne had a car so they had transportation once they were in town, with Kevin and Tim still taking the bus back and forth from Great Lakes.

They did try to promote every ploy to get their new girlfriends back to the hotel rooms, but Suzanne and Megan had really just met them and they didn't seem at the point to be ready for that kind of temporary physical commitment, or even for a serious long-term relationship – they were young, but they were also curious.

They had made some petting progress in Suzanne's car, tame as that was, by taking turns driving, with the other couple enjoying themselves in the back seat.

At least Kevin and Tim were having some real female human contact, more than most of the guys at the base.

The next to last weekend of "A" school, Kevin and Tim were invited by the women to see their university campus.

They showed them where they went to school, then they went cruising around, taking turns necking in the back seat.

After dinner at a local diner, the women made a very subtle, mutual big decision, by suggesting that they drive back to the hotel in Milwaukee.

Parking on the street, they found a liquor store nearby and purchased two bottles of wine. They stopped at a grocery store and picked up some crackers and cheese.

Walking into the hotel lobby, and although chatting lightly, they realized that not only was this going to be a big step in their relationships, but that this was probably the last time that they would be together, since school graduation was closing in.

Kevin had made no promises to keep in contact with Suzanne, neither had she with him. He wasn't feeling realistic about a long term future and Suzanne had college to finish. As in the 1942 movie, "Casablanca," he was going to places where she couldn't follow, and Suzanne could not chart her potential opportunities or relationships. These were fragile times during the war, as in all wars. This evening, however, was going to be a passionate, lasting remembrance.

They went to their respective rooms, and the couples settled in for the night. They spent comfortable and meaningful hours together.

Early the next morning, having used the rooms to their mutual satisfaction, Kevin and Tim walked the women to the car. It was a poignant, tender parting.

"Suzanne, this has been such a wonderful, special few weeks," Kevin said. "I had a really great time with you. You are such a nice person, but you know how it is, we're leaving, and you and Megan will still be here at school."

"This is like a textbook war romance, isn't it?" she said. "You know, Kevin, I really had a very nice time with you. We had a lot of fun, and I'm glad we had our fling. Don't worry about me. It was my time to take the next step. I'm a big girl. I really knew all along that this couldn't last," she went on. "It was just good the way it was, and I hope you take care of yourself."

"I will, and I hope you do well in school and land that big job. I'm glad this is going to be a sweet, and not a sour goodbye."

"Sure thing. Goodbye, Kevin, you take it easy." They kissed one long, last time.

Tim and Megan seemed to be going through the same situation. When they drove off in Suzanne's car, Kevin and Tim waved, and walked into the bus station to travel back to the base. Kevin wasn't about to swoop Suzanne up out of college and carry her away with him to follow the fleet – nor was she in any way expecting such a thing.

In sync with the phone call that had started this adventure, they just now about hung up on each other. It was mutual, gentle, and inevitable. It was the nature of Kevin and Tim's adventurous, independent, and transitory life at that time, and the combined youth of the four of them that couldn't possibly have sustained carrying on this relationship beyond their being at Great Lakes for these three months.

Having these weekends of social contact, romance, and mild love, and then how it led to intimacy was remarkable, indeed.

It had been fairly bold of Suzanne and Megan to continue to meet with these sailors, but apparently, they had been expectant in embracing this life experience.

It certainly made Kevin's and Tim's stay at the Training Center particularly unique, and altogether spectacular. This was definitely Class "A" school.

Six & Six

Jack Sorenson stood at the edge of the hatch in the vestibule leading to the forward fire room, and looked straight down the thirteen-foot ladder that landed on the upper level deck plates. He could almost see the 140° F heat waves of seemingly liquid air rising from the space. He was just about to go below to start the next cycle of his watch – six hours on, then the noon meal, also known as dinner, then six hours off, before repeating the cycle starting at 0-hundred hours, or midnight. He shared this watch with the other E-3 Boiler Tender Fireman already below on watch, Doyle Redding.

On this U.S. Navy destroyer, maintaining a speed of "Slow Ahead" to maneuver on Yankee Station in the Gulf of Tonkin off the coast of Vietnam, now in the spring of 1972, Jack had to face this grueling watch of six straight hours of carrying a clipboard through this engineering compartment containing two, one-story high boilers generating 1,200 lbs. per square inch of 900° F superheated steam, and all of the other machinery required to run the ship's main engines and generators.

He would be taking two-dozen bearing temperature and oil pressure readings of steam-driven pumps and fans, and checking the lubricating oil in the sumps of these machines.

Somewhat less technical, but just as vital, Jack would also be making coffee, taking out the sometimes seventy-five pound fully loaded trash barrel from below, straight up that ladder, with the help of any other sailor, either pushing it up as he was beneath it, or pulling it from the top of the ladder with a rope line, and then waking his watch relief.

Since Jack and Doyle were at the lowest end of the totem pole, they were also responsible, along with other selected E-4 / 3rd Class Petty Officers, to perform cleaning of firesides and watersides in the boilers. These operations, conducted following approximately six-hundred hours of steaming time, about every four months, involved dismantling a boiler's internal and external fittings, then climbing into the sometimes still quite warm 90^0 F cottage-sized fire box, to manually wire brush the soot from the exposed surfaces of hundreds of the steel tubes. With only two 100-watt drop lights for illumination, it was several hours' worth of a process of exhausting, filthy work brushing in the semi-darkness, leaving the sailors assigned to this task covered with choking, grimy soot.

In tandem with cleaning the fireboxes, the interiors of the stacks, or chimneys, above each of the boilers needed to be wire-brushed clean. This operation was frightening and miserable. Hanging on to a ladder mounted to one side of the 4'-0" x 3'-0" rectangular stack with one hand, wire brush in the other, and a rag tied around one's face, since it was barely breathable in there, a sailor would climb step by step two stories above the boiler.

Periodically, one would move a drop light hooked onto the ladder step by step toward the top pf the stack. This would barely illuminate the interior of this soot-blackened vertical tunnel – it was dark and frightening.

The stacks could not be cleaned with a hose, since water mixing with the soot would create sulfuric acid – sweat mixed with soot on a sailor's skin produced the same result. It was completely wretched while performing this task.

Cleaning watersides was equally unpleasant. Climbing into the steam drum, an approximately twelve-foot long, by approximately four-foot diameter steel cylinder, the sailors assigned to this task would lay on their backs and stomachs to remove all of the internal fittings and belly plates, using wrenches and hammers to loosen the nuts holding these parts in place.

This would expose the open ends of the one, two and four-inch diameter water tubes, which the sailors would then hand-push a pneumatically operated brush through every tube to remove any deposits developed from the steam bubbling through the water. It was dimly lit, cramped, hot and noisy. These operations also took several hours to complete.

The boiler then needed to be put back together, filled with water, and hydrostatically tested for leaks at 2,000 lbs. per square inch of pressure. Once it was determined that there were no leaks, then the boiler would be fired up to reset the safety valves.

The safety valves were located on top of the boilers, in the searing 180° F heat up there, and a spring would be manually adjusted by turning a fitting with a large screwdriver, to have each one of the valves pop at a designated relief pressure.

As hot as it was up there on those darkened metal-grated catwalks just above the tops of the boilers, the men wore their working bluejackets in an attempt to limit burns from leaning onto any of the scorching hot steel angle irons, railings or sections of un-insulated piping or valves. It was a dangerous, terrifying task, just another one in a long list of other equally dreadful operations.

Although Jack had written home to his family about his experiences while serving on this ship, even for these now short three months, no written description could fully do it justice regarding the time spent, and work performed.

The ships operating in the Western Pacific during the war were short-staffed for personnel to serve in the fire rooms, and many of them relied on a two-section watch for Messenger, those sailors responsible for performing the lowest and most mundane, but critical, functions of monitoring the boiler plants.

Jack and Doyle had been standing these exhausting watches now for the past three months, desperately hoping for another fireman to come aboard, so that they could go to a three-section watch underway, of four hours on and eight hours off, with a regular eight-hour work day in between. Although no matter how it was cut, even a three-section watch would translate to a sixteen-hour work schedule.

This is what these Boiler Tender sailors, and most of the rest of the crew on this ship faced, although with the addition of a third body there would be a semblance of sleep time mixed in.

Unfortunately, however, any sleep time was impacted while on the gun-line by the relentless BOOM! BOOM! BOOM! of the ship's main five-inch diameter gun, which would be fired sometimes almost non-stop for nights and days on end.

The ship was providing gunfire support for troop operations on the ground in-country, in order to curb North Vietnamese aggression across the demilitarized zone

While on this current underway deployment, as the war was escalating for another run, the ship was firing on, and near, the city of Quang Tri, one of the provincial capitals.

Jack had been able to secure several issues of *Vigilance*, a magazine published by ComCruDesPac (Commander, Cruiser / Destroyer Pacific Force, Seventh Fleet), which highlighted unclassified activities, and accomplishments of ships, and personnel in the cruiser / destroyer force.

As reported in these issues, the ship that Jack was serving on had been responsible, for example, of silencing enemy mortars two miles southwest of the city, for causing various explosions three miles northwest of that area, for destroying enemy emplacements seven miles north of there, for causing sustained fires and for destroying three bunkers four miles northwest.

They also destroyed other targets while serving on the gun line which generally included railroad yards, warehouses, coastal highways, airfields and surface to air (SAM) missile sites.

In addition, even before Jack had come aboard, while he was in transit to Japan leaving Travis Air Base outside of San Francisco, he had read, and had seen a photograph of, in a copy of the *Stars & Stripes*, essentially the Navy's system-wide home-town newspaper, that a sister ship to the one he was going to join had been involved in action. While engaged in providing gunfire support against coastal artillery, the ship had avoided an exploding shell fired by the North Vietnamese on the island of Hon Ne. Also in the article, related to this activity, eighteen-hundred sorties had been flown over Vietnam from air craft carriers, with seven planes lost, just during May, 1972. It had been a long and busy war so far, and he was headed into it.

He had also read that there were at least six air craft carriers, five cruisers, and more than thirty-five destroyers and destroyer escorts operating in the Gulf, hosting approximately forty-thousand Navy officers and crew. In addition, the *Stars & Stripes* reported that at this time during the war, United States Secretary of Defense Melvin Laird announced that thirty-five thousand men would be drafted by the end of the current year. This represented about half of the number that were drafted the previous year. It was clear to Jack that he was completely in the middle of a very active military conflict.

As a result of Jack's ship direct actions, and for other selected operations while he was on board, he and the crew were recipients of the Navy's Meritorious Unit Commendation awarded by the Chief of Naval Operations, for their efforts against enemy offensives, by providing accurate and timely gunfire support. They had accomplished vital engagements in partnership with other units of the armed forces.

As Jack would read several years later in the book "The Bridge at Dong Ha," written by John Miller, which described the effectiveness of providing off-shore gunfire support, this bridge in particular was notable for the heavy enemy traffic crossing it from North Vietnam into South Vietnam. The effort to cross this bridge during Easter of 1972 was halted because it was destroyed by the Marines, with additional naval gunfire support, as directed by the Marines. They all played their part, just like in any war.

In order to maintain this pace of gunfire support, the ship would need to take on armaments, or re-arm, about every third or fourth night. The ammunition that was used for this main gun mount was the 74-lb. projectile, which of course, the sailors called "bullets." These shells also needed 47-lb. powder charges in order to fire them.

Every sailor rated E-5 / 2nd Class Petty Officer and below had to carry both of these items, one at a time, from the pallets landing on the aft flight deck or from an amidships weather deck to the forward magazine below the gun while cradling each one like a baby without holding onto handrails.

Depending on how many pallets were received, each sailor on this work detail would carry three or four of each of the projectiles and powder charges every time that this operation was conducted, which usually took about two hours to complete.

And the operation was usually conducted under cover of darkness, with the only topside lights shining dimly through small, red globes, as the ship was either pitching and rolling in moderate seas, or while calm, steaming at approximately fifteen knots while tethered to the supply ship. It was tiring, and dangerous. Both Jack and Doyle, although holding a low-enough rate to participate in these evolutions, were exempt since they were on six and six.

They were standing watches almost non-stop while operating the plant, with their only authorized sleep time when out of the fire room. Not being on the re-armament detail was a small consolation for the relentless hours spent in that space in front of, around, and on top of the boilers.

Jack had arrived on board this ship at the age of twenty-three. He was a 5'-6" tall medium-built sailor with short blond hair, blue eyes, and a full beard. When he arrived, he weighed a solid 160 lbs. Now these three months later, he had shaved his beard off to stop the heat from virtually broiling his thick blanket of hair, and had lost 15 lbs. He felt alright; he was just tired most of the time, as was Doyle.

Although they did have a chance to sleep, or otherwise to be out of the fire room for selected periods, sometimes these respites were interrupted by something that they could not skip - General Quarters, or battle stations, usually due to an unidentified incoming contact picked up by radar.

This emergency condition was called several times while this ship was out there, mainly during a really lonely period of the night, like at 0300 hours or thereabouts.

As the distinctive loud bonging of the alarm bell jolted the sleeping sailors out of their racks, and snapped to sharp alertness those who were already awake, the Boiler Tenders raced to the fire rooms, or the Machinist Mates to the engine rooms. Other crew members ran to designated spaces throughout the ship, crossing paths with each other.

Jack, or Doyle, depending on which one of them was on watch at the time, would join the other watch standers, or those between watches, who had also arrived in the fire room.

The new arrivals would pour their cups of coffee from the constantly maintained electric pot next to the boiler control console. The men would stand together between the boilers in the firing alley on the lower level of either the forward or after fire rooms, at the usual temperature in these areas of 110° F, thirteen feet below the surface of the seawater surrounding the hull, waiting to see if they would live through the impending attack, or if they would die in the next few moments from a bomb explosion or by missile fire.

They had good reason to be worried. The North Vietnamese / Viet Cong were shooting live ammunition, and they were also sending fighter aircraft against the ships on the gun line.

Several minutes would go by as they stood there with their coffee, some talking with each other, some not saying anything. Fortunately, for the sailors on this ship on this night, the danger passed, as it was identified as non-threatening. The ship secured from General Quarters. Those that could went back to their racks to continue their sleep; those that couldn't, continued standing their watches. It was just another night in the war.

Some nights, those getting off watch at midnight, including either Jack or Doyle, would go topside aft to the darkened fantail to sit on the deck for a while to watch the fireworks. That is, seeing the shells from the ship's gun bursting on shore as they reached their targets of military or other installations, military vehicles, troop movements, or civilians. While on deck the sight of the exploding ordinance was as spectacular as the description of the rocket's red glare could be imagined in the *"Star Spangled Banner."* And the sound of the firing gun was much louder topside on the weather decks than it was when heard below within the ship.

The sailors never talked about what they were involved with in this war – they were just in it. Talking about the war, or protesting the war, was an indulgence afforded to those not in it, or for those whom had already served, and lived through it.

Jack and the others made comments about the stunning display of combat, and griped about the work that they had to do to accomplish this, however, no one out there ever made any mention of the political or social implications of these activities.

As E-3 firemen, Jack and Doyle did not have much choice in their watch stations, unless another E-3 would come on board, but they did have a choice to advance in their rating, by studying the technical manuals in anticipation of being recommended to take the advancement tests.

Achieving E-4 / 3rd Class Petty Officers, equivalent to Army Corporals, would mean that they would not usually stand Messenger watches on six and six. This would stop the relentless misery of what felt like almost a constant watch. In tandem with advancement in rate, 3rd Class POs usually advanced to the next level of responsibility for operating the boilers, that of Burnerman, which involved lighting off the boilers and monitoring the flames in the fireboxes, and the fuel delivery systems.

This next level watch was usually also in three sections of four hours on and eight hours off, with a regular eight hour work day in-between.

It was a relief to advance in rate, but not every sailor advanced. Most of the "B" Division sailors, and many of the sailors in other ratings, would remain at E-3 for their entire four-year enlistment.

It was few who studied the technical manuals, the military instructions, took their written and practical examinations, and were recommended to be advanced to E-4, and fewer still to E-5 / 2nd Class Petty Officer, equivalent to an Army Sergeant.

As Jack stood there this day at the edge of the hatch staring below into the excruciating heat of the fire room, he was more on the edge of wrenching a decision from deep within himself to end this nightmare right now. He didn't know how he could continue to face what was below. The heat, the work, the noise, the helpless hopelessness of his situation was overwhelming. He had a momentary image of pitching himself head-first down that ladder, to crash and die quickly as a pile of broken bones on the deck plates below.

He had never experienced such a depth of despair and misery as this, knowing that he would have to face this environment for the next several years. Nothing had prepared him for this raw, intense inferno that had enveloped him in severe physical, and emotional dismay. He was frightened, confused, and depressed. He needed to end it right now. It was the most terrifying moment that he had ever spent with himself. He was a finger hold away from suicide.

Fortunately, at that very moment of almost completely giving up he also had a critically revealing, strengthening vision of where he was hoping to go in his life and, as horrifying as this current situation was, it would only be temporary.

It was a split-second resolve that made him want to get past this devastating moment, realizing that he would get through this, that he did have things to look forward to, socially, and for future civilian employment. He gripped the handle welded to the bulk-head for a few seconds, thinking more about how he couldn't just ignore this commitment to himself to achieve success, and a future life by ending it all here. He had to go on.

He took another breath, stepped over the hatch rim and climbed down the ladder. He was calmer now, and proceeded to resume the obligations to himself and as a sailor in the steam ship Navy. Following this personal confrontation and self-resolve, after several more months he was closer to having enough time in his rate of E-3 to move on.

He had been diligently studying, and had been recommended to take the E-4 examination. He was hopeful that he would be advanced even before a new fireman would arrive, easing the burden of six and six.

During the next month, a new man did come aboard, and Jack and Doyle's purgatory, at least for standing watches, was over.

Following a brief training period for the new sailor, they immediately went to four hours on, and eight hours off, except for working hours, and their lives were marginally better. Although they sometimes got more sleep, this was still only captured between the interruptions of daily work, multiple watches, and nightly war.

During the next three months, Jack and Doyle passed their written and practical examinations, and were promoted to 3rd Class Petty Officers. They were no longer messengers but would continue additional training in operating the burners and other equipment.

There was a neatly painted sign hanging in the forward and after fire rooms, paraphrasing Winston Churchill's quotation from World War II, and written with a smirk - "Never have so few done so much for so little."

Six and six might have come to an end for them, but the agony of the ubiquitous "twenty-four and carry on" was still the rule for sea duty as the war dragged on to its conclusion during the next eighteen months. Standing his watches, and working through those exhausting days and nights kept Jack completely occupied during all times at sea. He would note the end of the war on one of his mid-watches, when the ship's gun stopped firing.

Puke

Ben Spooner, a U.S. Navy 2nd Class Petty Officer, the rate of an Army Sergeant, watched as the sweat rolled down the plump face of Fireman Apprentice Allen Pute. He looked like a glistening wet statue as he stood there in his sweat-stained, rumpled dungaree uniform, staring through the peep hole at the 3,000° F oil-fired flames roaring in the one-story high firebox of # 2A boiler. His appearance matched the nickname that had been bestowed on him soon after he had reported to the boiler room on this Navy destroyer – "Puke."

Nicknames were prevalent among the crew, with the most common ones shortening of one's last name, or otherwise, highlighting some feature of one's physical presence or personality. For example, there was Felix "Tommy" Thompson, a former steel worker, Dominick "Bull" Anton, a pipe fitter in civilian life, Ted "Wheels" Singleton, previously a car mechanic, and the big guy, Drayton "House" Ferris, a former print shop foreman.

Ben had invariably acquired the handle, "Gentle Ben," from a popular television show at the time, however, the men didn't call him that to his face.

Ben was a twenty-five year old, 5'-8" tall block of a man with blonde hair cut to standard military length, clean-shaven, with a square face containing dark blue eyes.

He did not look at all gentle, although he was fair and helpful to his men. Ben was a competent engineer and mechanic, a sailor who believed in what he was doing in the military. He was used to supervising, and contributing to the well-being of the men who worked for him, and with whom he was serving.

Allen, a squat 5'-4" nineteen-year old with short fuzzy brown hair and pin-set brown eyes, had his nickname culled from his last name, Pute, but not altogether derived from the sound or spelling of it. He had earned this disgusting name because of his attitude and work performance. The dull expression on his face seemed to indicate little ambition or interest in his rating.

Ben thought about Allen's first day in the fire room three months before, when he descended the almost vertical thirteen-foot ladder to the upper level deck plates, then the eight-foot more angled ladder to the lower level, backwards.

A sailor was supposed to walk down a ladder like that facing forward, so that one could see what was below, and to balance oneself in rolling and pitching seas. On this first day, though, in port, the ship was not moving, and the boilers were not firing.

"Allen Pute, Fireman Apprentice, reporting," he had said to no one in particular.

"I know your name," Frank "Beef" Atkinson, the large-framed 1st Class Petty Officer answered him irritably. "We were all on the fantail this morning for quarters, don't you remember?"

Frank's response was not altogether warranted, since Allen had innocently stated his arrival, but Frank was sometimes just ornery.

"I was just saying what I thought you were supposed to say," Allen mumbled.

"Don't you be thinking now, Pute, get you in trouble," Stephen Grant, one of the 3rd Class Petty Officers standing nearby said to him jokingly.

Some of the other crew members laughed. That should have been the moment for Allen to join in the humor, to say something friendly, to be in on the ribbing, but he just stood there. The crew in this fire room was a tight, exclusive group, very judgmental, and they formed their opinions of new members almost immediately. A new man had to prove himself quickly. Allen had not made much of an impression.

That first day of Allen's arrival, Brad Sontag, one of the supervising 3rd Class Petty Officers, handed out work assignments. "All right everyone, listen up. Joey and Steely, we need the oil changed in # 2 air compressor. Peaches and Smitty, take the booster pump coupling replacement." As he finished assigning work, Allen stood there with uncertainty.

Some new men might have taken the initiative and asked Brad what they should do since he hadn't been given a specific task, but Allen had not seized the opportunity. Ben had seen other new men face up to being in a new situation, and had seen others who did not handle it very well.

He wanted to give Allen the benefit that he was just shy and might come around. Unfortunately, Allen's next reaction dashed this hope.

Brad said evenly, "Pute, I want you to get a set of gloves from that locker over there, a paint scraper, and a bucket. Go to the corner near # 1 fuel pump and lift up a deck plate, then crawl in, make yourself comfortable, and start cleaning out the muck in that section of the bilges. You can come up for air in about an hour to grab a smoke, so let's get started."

Allen had looked blankly at Brad. He was supposed to have known, as everyone else in the Navy knew, that all new sailors assigned to the engineering spaces started out by cleaning the bilges.

Once the steam plant was operational and they were at sea, in addition to various house-cleaning and painting tasks, Allen would be trained in the first basic watch standing assignment of a new fireman - Messenger.

The tasks, and responsibilities on this watch included making regularly scheduled rounds of the plant, checking the oil levels in various machines, and recording machinery temperature and pressure readings.

For now, while at cold iron, he would have to spend some time with his nose figuratively either to the massive keel of the ship or to the longitudinal steel ribs while cleaning bilges, or he would be assigned to scrape and paint something.

Allen didn't move. Instead of answering Brad with a snappy, or even a reluctant, "Aye, Aye," he said petulantly, "I don't really want to clean bilges. I've got on clean dungarees. Why don't you give me something else to do?"

Brad and Ben looked at each other, surprise mirrored on their faces. Non-rated Firemen Apprentices did not say these things to Petty Officers. Several of the crew still standing there waited for the hammer to fall.

"Listen up, Pute," Brad continued evenly, but with an edge, "you get yourself out of my face, grab your gear and put your fat little body into those bilges now for the next hour or two. Sass back at me again on this, and once you get under those deck plates you will remain there for the rest of your enlistment. Do you understand what I'm saying?"

Allen's pink, mushy face brightened to red. No one else moved. "Okay," he said, "But I'm not going to like it."

"Look, snipe," Brad hissed, "I don't care what you like. This isn't your first day in the Navy. You're going to do what you're told when you're told. If you behave yourself while attached to this gang, you may improve your lot in life."

Ben piped in, "Listen to what he's saying, my man. Everyone pulls his own weight down here, and we're a team. You got to start at the bottom. I thought you had this figured out from Boot Camp."

Brad added, "You know sailor, from now on, we're going to call you 'Puke,' until you can be worthy of getting your real name back. That's all bud, now get going."

Puke's little eyes had widened and his back went stiff. Now he looked like a hot, frightened, pumpkin. He turned and walked toward the tool locker.

Ben agreed with Brad, and thought that Allen deserved his new name for not having the sense to bond with this group. He felt uneasy, though, about having to rely on a guy like Puke in the ensuing period when they would be at sea operating the plant in the ship's combat role.

If Puke was slow to react, and was uncooperative as a worker, Ben wasn't sure how he would rise to the responsibilities of being part of the action team needed to keep the plant going during operations.

"Hey, we better keep an eye on this guy," Brad said to Ben.

"I'm hoping we can change his attitude as we go along," he answered.

"I don't know. I think it'll just get worse. He's not our kind of people," Frank added.

"We have to hope," Ben countered. "I'm not going to ride him too hard while we're in port; maybe that will help."

"All right, I'll stay out of the way for a while, too," said Frank.

"Okay, then, let's see if I can help him see the light," Ben said.

During the next two weeks while the ship was still tied to the pier, even though Ben made the effort to include Allen, Puke did not respond very well. Ben would just have to wait until they got underway to see if he would either continue to fail in adversity, or if he would recover, and would succeed when faced with the chance to prove himself.

Following their in-port repair time, now that they were at sea with the plant at full steam, it was deafeningly noisy in the fire room. Here, below the waterline just beyond the hull, and a few feet above the keel in the murky depths of the bilges, steam was produced for the main engines, the generators, and the auxiliaries. They were on Yankee Station in the Gulf of Tonkin, 20,000 yards off the coast of Vietnam in 1972 during the waning days of the war, within the effective range of the ship's main gun, and just out of range of most of the ordinance being fired back at them.

At 110° F, the temperature on the lower level of the space was at least 30° F cooler than on the upper level where the grated catwalks provided access to the boiler water feed pumps, the forced draft blowers, and the air compressors. This was cooler still, though, than the 180° F temperature on top of the boilers where some of the men were scraping paint at this very moment. Their only relief from the heat were huge "elephant trunks," the flexible tubes blowing air directly on them, tapped from the topside fresh air intake fans.

It took a tremendous effort of labor, and of eating several finger-fulls of salt tablets throughout the sixteen-hour workdays while underway to just stand one's watches.

They also needed to perform selected cleaning, to polish brass, or to effect minor repairs, and to sometimes have to face the additional burden of responding immediately to emergency work. They did this while standing their watches in the four-person team consisting of the Top Watch on the lower level for the boiler controls, the Check Watch on the upper level for the feed pumps and boiler water, the Burner Watch on the firebox flames and fuel oil pumps, and the Messenger taking readings throughout the fire room, making coffee and waking the next watch section.

It was almost inconceivable that humans could work in these conditions of heat, humidity, and noise, but they did, while the blood in their veins seemed to thin out to the viscosity of hot motor oil running through a race car engine.

The fire room crew was made up of sailors of a range of technical abilities who faced their environment with varying levels of acceptance and complaint. They were enlisted men, almost only property, but skilled in steam plant operations, or learning the skills that were required.

During one of his two daily four-hour watches, Ben turned the corner at # 2A boiler, and he immediately saw a stream of steaming water shooting out from the automatic valve which controlled the speed and capacity of the pump used for fighting fires.

There was no question that this repair could not wait - the pump was critical to the ship's safety and operational readiness. The ship was responsible for retrieving fighter pilots who might have crashed into the sea following raids on shore targets, flying from the aircraft carrier that the destroyer was assigned to guard for several hours, or several days. Having the ability to fight any on-board fires during these operations was not debatable – they had to be ready.

On the days when they were not plane guarding, on-board fire fighting was just as crucial. When not chasing carriers, the ship provided gunfire support for South Vietnamese troop operations, for this operation, just south of Quang Tri City, near the demilitarized zone. Sometimes the Viet Cong would shoot back at them. The ship had been hit with shrapnel on two occasions during this past fifty-four days while underway; they had been operating just a bit too close to the beach. Although the hits had not resulted in causing any on-board fires, the capability to contain them could not be compromised.

During these gunfire operations, some members of the crew would be at their work stations while some of them would be standing watches – normal routine. Sometimes, however, especially in the middle of the night, known as "zero dark thirty," the ship's entire crew would be at General Quarters, or Battle Stations, when the radar in Combat Information Center (CIC) picked up an unidentified contact.

A contact could be an enemy aircraft or missile, things that could kill them, on its way directly toward the ship with the engineering spaces as prize target areas. In all cases, this fire pump needed to function properly.

Since this pump casualty was taking place on Ben's watch, he would be accountable for implementing corrective action since he was one of the supervising Petty Officers. This repair would need to be completed while they were steaming full speed ahead, plowing through the water at more than twenty-five knots just aft of the carrier.

He walked across the deck plates, and said to Frank, the 1st Class senior supervisor on this watch, "Looks like the diaphragm and gasket in the fire pump governor are shot. I've got to shut it down and take it off the line."

Frank picked up the 5J circuit phone, and called the forward engine room, Main Control, to explain conditions. A minute later, the Chief Engineer, Lieutenant Andrew Hardin, climbed down the two ladders to the lower level of the fire room.

"Beef, Ben, what's it going to take to get this back to readiness?" he asked them. He respected his Petty Officers for their knowledge of the plant.

"Sir, if we can just isolate that pump for maybe about two hours, Ben here can make the repair," Beef said.

Ben agreed. "We can fix this pretty fast. I've done this one before, though not under these circumstances while plane guarding."

"Alright," Lt. Hardin said, "I'll inform the Captain on the Bridge. I'll let you fellows know when to proceed. Let's keep the 5J circuit clear between Main Control, and you." This was standard procedure during operations.

Lt. Hardin left the space and went above. Frank said to Ben, "Who do you want to work with?"

Ben thought about his usual workers who were always dependable. He considered that either Tommy, or Dominick, or anyone of the boiler gang were competent and knew what they were doing technically. He was confident that each one of them would be fine for this repair.

Then he thought about Puke. He was just now working in the overhead above the exhaust steam condenser on the upper level, scraping, and painting the angle iron supports.

Unfortunately, Puke had not improved as much as Ben had hoped he would since getting underway. For example, Ben had been told by one of the non-rated men about the need to sometimes have to wake Allen a second time from sleep since he didn't spring into action to relieve the watch. This was unacceptable – every watch stander was entitled to be relieved at fifteen minutes before the hour of their next four-hour watch. Puke's nickname continued to fit, not only mimicking his real name, but from his persistent personal shortcomings, and poor behavior.

As a senior Petty Officer, however, Ben felt responsible for bringing Allen into the fold by treating him with respect, and including him on repair operations, as part of his training.

Puke was already standing his watches as a Messenger, and had been warned several times, even during Boot Camp, about the absolute rule to never "radio" the readings on the equipment. This was a situation where a sailor would skip a task, and fabricate the current temperature or pressure level of a part of a machine or system. This action was beyond the pale of negligence – it was dangerous to the point of life-threatening. Fortunately, it did not seem that Puke had shirked on his performance in this regard. He was just resistant to, or didn't understand what being cooperative was about.

Even today, while most of the others in the gang didn't like what they were assigned to do, they might have grumbled amongst themselves, but they didn't complain to their supervisor. Puke had whined straight back to his senior Petty Officer about having to work in the heat, just as he had complained when he first arrived on board. It didn't make any difference. The work had to get done, and these boiler room sailors had to do it.

Ben was willing to continue to have Puke try to redeem himself. He could have chosen any one of his men; instead, he answered Frank, "I'll take Puke."

Frank didn't seem surprised. He knew what Ben had in mind. "Okay, have one of the guys call Puke to come below; we've got a job for him."

Ben asked one of the men to get Puke. He had extricated himself from the engulfing tangle of steel, and presented himself to Ben and Beef on the lower level.

Ben said, "Allen, the fire pump needs a diaphragm. I want you to learn something new, and to have a hand in something important. You up for that? You know we have to be ready to put out a fire immediately or to wash down any fuel spill while we're chasing this carrier."

It seemed plain to Ben, and Frank that Puke was surprised and grateful. Allen said, "Me? That sure beats scraping paint."

"Okay, then, what do you think we'll need, and what's a diaphragm?" Ben asked him.

Puke hesitated. Ben knew he had some previous basic training in shipboard mechanics. Ben waited. Then Puke said tentatively, "We'll need slugging wrenches to fit those flange nuts, and a hammer." After a thoughtful pause, he continued, "We'll need new gasket material, a scraper, and a drift pin; I mean a marlinspike." He went on, "The diaphragm? It's a steel disc to hold the steam supply pressure against spring tension to maintain the pump speed. That's right?"

"That's good, Allen. Sounds like you've been paying attention around here. Also, let's grab snips to cut the gaskets, some white lead paste, and some crocus cloth. Anything else?" he asked.

Puke looked at Ben. "I know, how about a screwdriver?"

"You got it," Ben said. "Now let's get going."

They opened the locker above the tool bench to get their materials, and pulled tools from the large drawer, and from the cabinet beneath the bench. They walked across the deck plates to the pump.

"Go ahead and shut down the steam supply, exhaust, and sea water intake and pump discharge valves," Ben said.

"The ship won't have fire main pressure on the port side. We've got to work fast. We could need that pump anytime." Puke said.

"Good thinking, buddy." He was impressed with Puke's enthusiasm.

They loosened the bolts holding the top section of the valve and removed it, then hammered the flange nuts loose, with Puke holding the wrenches. They removed the 40 lb. valve, and lowered it to the deck plates. Puke dried the surfaces; then he cleaned them and the line flanges with crocus cloth, a smooth metal sandpaper used for polishing. He took the diaphragm out of its package and set it in place.

"Let me make the gaskets," Allen said. "I can hammer on things."

"Spoken like a true BT. Go right ahead."

Puke cut two pieces of gasket material large enough to cover each face of the flange, then hammered the gasket edges with the ball-peen hammer to cut them into the matching shape to fit.

They lifted the valve back in place. Puke lined up the flanges with the drift pin, placed the bolts in the holes and tightened the nuts by hammering on the short-handled box-end slugging wrench.

Ben said, "That's good, you tightened them in sequence."

"Sure, I did think of that."

Ben asked, "Okay, what would you do next?"

"I'd open the pump suction and discharge, and cut in cooling water to the shaft packing glands."

"You're thinking sharp here," Ben said.

They tested for leaks by opening the exhaust valve, then cracked open the steam supply, letting in 600 pounds per square inch of 500° F steam.

They inspected the flanges for leaks. "Everything looks good to me," Ben said. "Let's bring the discharge pressure up. You adjust the spring. Watch your gauge."

Puke used the large screwdriver to adjust the spring tension until the pump was up to speed. Although it had been a fairly straightforward repair, it was potentially hazardous under emergency conditions. It had taken them about two hours as estimated.

While they were cleaning up, Ben asked, "What did you do before the Navy?"

"Well, I'm from a small town in Pennsylvania. I didn't do much except help my dad plant soybeans. We had a lot of acres. After I graduated from high school, I didn't have a chance to go anywhere out of the county, so I joined up, but I didn't really want to."

"I just didn't want to get drafted into the Army. I'm really glad you let me work with you. No one likes to work with me since I sometimes don't get things right."

"Well, you did okay for me," Ben reassured him. "You looked like you knew what you were doing. It was a good job."

They walked across the deck plates to Frank. "Pump tested and on the line," Ben reported.

Frank contacted Main Control with this information, and Lt. Hardin reported satisfactory completion to the Bridge. He then came below to the fire room, and gave Puke and Ben the customary, ubiquitous Navy accolade, "Well done!"

The triumph today was hoped by Ben to be a positive turning point in Allen's personal, and professional development. Ben wasn't sure that the rest of Puke's time in the fire room would be totally stellar, but he was hopeful that his behavior might be adjusted.

Ben continued to put this method of personal inclusion into practice in various situations later in his Navy service. He found that just a little mentoring, and positive reinforcement could go a long way to helping someone improve themselves. Ben thought about what was more important than their success at this repair was the look on the face of Allen when they finished. Through the sweat and the grime, Puke was smiling.

Liberty Call

Pusan, South Korea. It was summer, 1972. For Dan Bronk, this was the first time for him in this seaport on this ship, a United States Navy destroyer just off from the gun line along the coast of Vietnam in the Gulf of Tonkin.

The ship had been on Yankee Station, a position based on coordinates approximately 20,000 yards out from the beach, about due east of Da Nang, just south of the demilitarized zone at the North Vietnamese border. The ship was providing shore gunfire support with the 5" / 54 caliber main gun, to sustain the actions of Army soldiers and Marines carrying out combat missions on the ground in-country. Sometimes the ship ran a little too close to the shore, and was the recipient of enemy shrapnel from Viet Cong ordinance fired back at them, but not too often. Although it was hot and dangerous on this ship in the Gulf, nothing could ever remotely compare to what was taking place for those troops in the jungle.

Dan was an E-5 Petty Officer Second Class, a rate equivalent to an Army sergeant. He was a Machinist Mate, responsible with the other sailors in "M" Division for running the steam-powered main engines, electrical generators and fresh water evaporators, amongst other equipment on this warship.

He was an unmarried twenty-seven year-old, of average height at 5'-9." He was thin, weighing one hundred seventy pounds, which made him seem taller. He had light skin, with his face framed by a sparse beard and a light mustache, punctuated by light blue eyes.

He had been in the Far East for only the past eight months, but had been in the Navy for more than five years, having transferred from a destroyer escort that was home ported in Norfolk, Virginia. That ship had then been deployed from Norfolk to various areas of the world for selected missions, around South America and through the Panama Canal.

The ship he was attached to now was forward deployed, that is, permanently home ported in the Far East, at the Naval base and shipyard in Yokosuka, Japan. This provided a constant availability for the ship to be on station off the coast of Vietnam, currently for the past two years. As they periodically came off the gun line, the ship had been fortunate to have pulled liberty in several ports in the Western Pacific.

The city of Pusan was a welcome liberty for the enlisted crew and officers for a short time following more than a month at sea. For the engineering department personnel, having worked in the heat and noise of the ship's engine rooms and fire rooms day and night, and for the Gunner's Mates who were firing onto the shore, it was exhausting, both for the crew and for the sleek, mechanical brute that was this destroyer.

They were all tired - the men, the ship, and they needed to spend some time in port after all of that gunfire, and after all of the chasing of aircraft carriers at more than twenty-five knots to perform plane guarding for the Navy pilots who were flying back "feet wet" from sorties over Vietnam,

Cruising out of the Gulf, through the Sea of Japan, into the South China Sea, and then arriving in Korea, they tied up to the pier in Pusan. Once they had tied up, the engineering plant, which consisted of the forward and after engine rooms, the two fire rooms containing the boilers, and various other spaces containing auxiliary equipment and systems, was able to be virtually shut-down.

In this port, they could connect to shore services at the pier for electricity, steam, fresh water, and did not have to run the main propulsion plant. Those officers and crew who were scheduled to remain on board for the first and second days of liberty were the cold iron watch, and could perform repair work that couldn't be completed while the plant was in operation. They were going to be in Pusan for the next four days, with liberty for all hands in two sections of forty-eight hours each.

Pusan was the largest city in South Korea. It was a very industrialized area, of steel manufacturing, textiles and shipbuilding. It had been the place that some of the fiercest fighting had taken place during the Korean War during 1950 through 1953. The city was now jointly controlled by the Korean Army, the Korean Ministry of Transportation, and the U.S. Army.

The city hosted a large military base occupied predominantly by U.S. Army and Marine personnel, who accommodated Navy sailors on liberty, and helped to contain the Merchant Marine sailors who also pulled into this busy commercial port.

Currency was the Won, at an exchange rate of about ₩ 400 to the U.S. $1.00. U.S. Greenbacks were not permitted to be used in the city, but could only be exchanged for Won, or for Military Payment Certificates (MPC) at the nearby United Seaman's Service Club, a location used by military personnel and Merchant Marine sailors. These currencies could not be converted back to U.S. dollars, so officers and crew were advised to exchange only what they thought they would spend while on the beach.

Typically, some of the crew didn't have much money in any form to start with, so it wasn't a big stretch not to convert very much money. Merchant seamen had more money than the Navy sailors, since they were civilian workers, and they provided competition against the Navy for the favors of the women in the bars.

It wasn't really much of a challenge to pair up with any of the hostesses in the clubs, no matter what your occupation was; you just needed a reasonable amount of money.

Navy personnel on ships or on shore duty were paid monthly in cash, however, one could specify how much money one wanted to be paid by filling out a "chit" on payday.

This would indicate how much to save, or how much was to be taken out of one's pay in advance for an allotment to be deposited remotely. Dan had an allotment being deposited in a bank account in the States, or back in the "world," as home was referred to by those serving in Vietnam, as if this wasn't a part of the world.

He currently had the expense of a motorcycle loan from the Navy Credit Union that he was paying off, but was basically fairly frugal with the pay that he had left. His motorcycle was parked back at the base in Yokosuka, and he would retrieve it when the ship went to its homeport. Although he was earning about $400 per month as an E-5 Petty Officer, plus $50 per month in combat pay, he usually had money in his pocket to go on liberty.

Up until this point in his Navy career, he had saved close to $6,000, which included money he had saved from his pay and from the $13,000, less taxes, that he had been paid for his reenlistment incentive. In those days of the war, the Navy was very anxious to keep their trained sailors on active duty since most enlisted sailors only stayed in the Navy for their first enlistment. It was hard to keep good technicians and military-minded personnel, hence the large cash incentives.

Dan's first focus for liberty whenever he went across the brow, or gangway of a ship at the Quarterdeck to go ashore, was to get an ice-cold beer in a cool, dark bar. His second order of business was to meet a hot woman, maybe in that same place, who could also cool him off.

He had accomplished these tasks in various other ports on the east coast of the United States, in various countries in Africa and during the past eight months while on board this ship, in Subic Bay, the Philippines and in Kaohsiung, Taiwan.

This day in Pusan, he left the ship with his steaming buddy, his good friend Chris, another 2nd Class Petty officer, and several other "M" and "B" Division sailors of various rates. At this time in the Navy, civilian clothes were authorized for liberty and each of them was dressed casually, but appropriately.

Taxicabs were available at the head of the pier for travel within the city, however, the drivers almost never had any change, so any payment with a bill above the cost of the fare would be the tip, although tipping was not a big custom here. Apparently, the taxi drivers just picked this practice up from this custom in the United States, performed here by U.S. military personnel. Buses could also be used, with travel between any two zones along the main streets costing ₩ 20 (about $.05). Not too many sailors took buses.

The sailors and Army personnel had also picked up a cultural detail from the Koreans — when waving to call someone over to them, like for instance to one of the hostesses from the bars, the hand was pointed fingers down, with palm waved towards the caller, rather than the hand pointed with fingers up to wave someone over.

It was an affectation that sailors and soldiers used in the bars, and in the streets as often as possible to show the hostesses that they were savvy and acculturated. Whether the hostesses were impressed with this wasn't very clear. Most hostesses just went with sailors or soldiers based on their ability to pay them money, and in the least, if they had the outward indication that they weren't going to be mean to them.

The sailors had from the time that they went on the beach for liberty until midnight to make this impression. The city had placed a restriction on the military, and on the general population, by the imposition of a curfew. Everyone absolutely had to be off of the streets by midnight. Being out there past that time was just not an option. There were armed military and Korean civilian police patrols monitoring this condition, ready to make arrests.

Either one met someone at a bar and went home with her, or went to a hotel, or one went back to the ship alone, or with some other buddies. Either way, one needed to be gone.

Chris and the others had been to Pusan twice before, since they had been on board this destroyer for about a year and a half. Dan was looking forward to wherever it was that they would end up. The small group climbed in to one cab.

Chris told the driver, "Seaman's Club," and the cab took off. They needed to change some money. It was a simple matter to do so while the cab waited for them.

Dan exchanged about $50.00 into Won – based on Chris's recommendation he figured this would be more than enough for the two days and nights that he had liberty. He kept another $10.00 in U.S. currency in his sock just in case, along with his cigarettes.

Leaving the club, it was a short ride to their next stop, the "Lucky Bar." The "Lucky Bar" shared the four-block long street with the other dozen or so bars that lined both sides of this enclave. The group disembarked from the cab. Someone paid the driver and they walked into the bar.

It was dark in there, but not as cool as Dan would have liked. Just as well, he and the other "M" and "B" division sailors were used to the usual 120° F to 140° F heat of the ship's engineering spaces anyway.

Leaning along the walls of the bar and sitting at some of the tables lining the walls were several hostesses, also known as "bar girls." They were dressed nicely, in casual dresses or skirts and blouses.

Although to Dan this was an inviting sight, what he really needed now was liquid refreshment – later for a date.

The group of sailors crossed the center dance floor and arranged themselves at the bar, sitting on stools. As they started to order their drinks, each of them was immediately paired by one of the hostesses who had crossed the floor.

"How are you doing?" Dan's new companion said to him in a friendly voice, in perfect English, with a slight accent.

"I'm okay," he smiled back at her.

"Can you buy me a Champagne Cocktail?" she asked

"Sure can," he said, and ordered a drink for the lady.

A Champagne Cocktail was just a glass of tea that only looked like an alcoholic drink, however, it cost just as much as one – a specialty of the house.

One of the factors contributing to the women holding onto their jobs was how many cocktails that they managed to have the sailors buy them. For each drink purchased, they collected a plastic disk from the bartender for counting later.

Chris and the others were having similar introductory conversations with the other women.

Once drinks were ordered and provided, the talk between couples was about travel, and this city, and where people lived and how long they had been in the Far East, without the sailors giving away too much detail.

The sailors were well-schooled and savvy in keeping military maneuvers and other tactical information away from strangers – after all, there was a war on. These sailors stationed in the mysterious Orient may have been somewhat casual in their attitudes, but they weren't stupid.

"So, what's your name?" Dan asked.

"I'm Helen. You like that name?"

"Yeah, that's nice," he said. "It's pretty, like you."

And to Dan, she was pretty. Standing about 5'-3" she was petite and slim with jet-black hair cut straight to the length of her neck, having the same shape as her bangs, with dark eyes, minimal make-up and red lipstick.

She seemed to be at least in her late thirties, much older than most of the other hostesses, who were basically in their late teens and early twenties, but Dan was fine with this.

He was already twenty-seven, older than many of the rest of the sailors in his division, having come into the Navy later than most, and now staying longer.

He had been with many women of his age and younger, and older. He just got along with most everyone and most women, and was not too concerned with age, just with how well a person behaved towards him. He felt relaxed, and anticipated that he and Helen would spend the rest of this day and then the evening together.

Spending friendly time together wasn't always so easy for all couples. Sometimes, just like meeting any new person, individuals clicked together, or they didn't.

Although being with a Navy or Merchant Marine sailor was business as usual for the hostesses, and they certainly were used to being attentive, and did cater to the needs of their new-found, temporary boyfriends, if it was completely uncomfortable there were plenty of other hostesses, and other sailors, to go around.

There wasn't usually too much fuss. Couples made it work basically no matter what, but in this situation, they did spend several hours and sometimes days together.

The relationship, though fleeting, could become a very sensitive, emotional event. Sometimes a sailor got married to one of these women. Other times it was purely mechanical.

"Are you from Pusan?" Dan asked her.

"No, from Chinhae," she answered. "Do you know where that is?"

"Yes, it's about forty miles west of here."

"Very good," she said. "You have been to Korea before?"

"No, my first time here. It's just that I know where it is."

"I came to Pusan about ten years ago. I never went back."

"Oh, is there something there that you need to go back to?"

"No, I came here with my daughter when she was a little girl and we live here now. Do you not like that I have a daughter, that I am a mother?"

"That's alright with me." Dan didn't think that he was headed to foster fatherhood immediately after meeting Helen so he wasn't overly concerned. It would have been somewhat unusual for a hostess to be married, but it could be that way.

"Is your husband back in Chinhae?"

"I don't know where he is," she said. "He was drinking too much, and went away to work. I don't know what happened to him after that."

"That's too bad," Dan said. "Any reason that you might be looking for an American husband?" He smiled at her. "I'm not volunteering, just asking."

"Only if that would be something that happened; otherwise I'm just a working girl."

Dan took a sip of his drink. "How old is your daughter?"

"Now she is twelve. She lives with my mother, not far from here, and goes to school."

"How far did you get in school?" he asked.

"Oh, I finished high school, then secretarial courses, but finding job is very hard."

"So you came here to the Lucky Bar?"

"Well, here and other bars," she said.

"That's okay, I know, it's hard to find work. For me, it's okay that you're here, so that I could meet you."

"That's nice, that you like me. How about you, how much in school did you go?"

Dan said, "Well, for me, I finished high school, then went to junior college for computer programming, but I never finished. I worked around for a while," he continued. "Once as a house painter, then an auto mechanic, and some other things, then while waiting for the draft I joined the Navy."

"Oh, yes, your military draft for the war. How about married?" she said, "Are you married?"

"No, never married, never even close," he answered.

"That's okay," she said, "Not everyone gets married. Sometimes married sailors come into the bars and take us girls out."

"I don't think that's right," Dan said, "If you're married, you shouldn't be fooling around."

"Yes," Helen said, "But you know, a guy could get lonely away from his wife out at sea and maybe wants to be with a woman."

"That doesn't matter, that a sailor is lonely," he answered. "If someone is married, the husband or wife needs to have respect for the person they're married to. If you're single, okay, so you can have quickies or go on dates and have overnights and have a steady girlfriend or boyfriend, but you can't do that if you're married."

"You know," she said, "you're a nice guy."

"Thanks, Helen. You are very nice, too."

"And how about movies, you like movies?" Helen asked him.

"Yes, I do," Dan said. "What do you have in mind?"

"If you want, we could see a movie," she said.

"Sounds good to me." He called over down the bar. "Hey Chris, you want to take a break and see a movie?" Chris was in close conversation with his new girlfriend.

"Sure," he said. He turned to the woman sitting next to him. "Brenda, how about it, you want to leave the bar and take in a movie?"

"Okay, we go now," Brenda said.

Helen and Brenda said goodbye to several of the other hostesses, gathered their handbags, and the four of them said goodbye to everyone else, and walked out to the sunlight. They went down the street to the corner and jumped in a cab.

Threading through the neighborhood for several blocks, the four of them chatted amicably about the sites in the street. They arrived at the theater, Dan paying the driver. Dan and Chris then bought movie tickets for each of them. They stopped at the candy counter and bought popcorn and sodas, then they went in to find seats.

There was nothing that different about going to the movies here in South Korea than it was in the United States – and with dates.

It was crowded, but no one seemed to pay any mind to the four of them – the people in the audience just seemed to be used to seeing Anglo men and Korean women coming to the movies, especially since the theater wasn't too far from the waterfront and the bar district.

What was decidedly different, though, was that the film did not start until everyone stood up and the South Korean National Anthem was played – they don't usually open films at movie theaters in the United States with the National Anthem, but they did here.

Another difference was what Dan had been warned about by Chris earlier in the cab ride on their way to the theater – the rats running through the seats. It was definitely true, as Dan stood there for the National Anthem a rat ran right against his leg.

Looking down, he could see several others scampering through the legs of the patrons. Dan wasn't exactly afraid of rats, but he certainly didn't like them. Sitting down, no other critters came close to any of the four of them, and they settled in to watch the movie. None of them placed their popcorn or sodas on the floor, but held them close during the entire film.

This was to be Dan's first viewing of a Bruce Lee film. It was, "The Way of the Dragon," Lee's second movie, in which he defends his relatives from mobsters while the family operates a Chinese restaurant in Rome.

His character is forced into having a fight to the death, which he wins, using his exquisite talents in Kung Fu fighting in the Coliseum with actor Chuck Norris playing the heavy, who was then the world Karate champion, and a rising film star himself.

This was a great movie, with clear cut heroes and villains. The movie was spoken in English dialogue with Korean subtitles, so Chris and he had little trouble following along, and neither did Helen and Brenda.

The audience at this showing was frenzied, cheering on their hero. Bruce Lee was a skyrocketing star at that time following his previous role as Kato in the "Green Hornet" television show a few years earlier, and from his first movie, "Enter the Dragon."

Once the movie was over, they left the theater, hailed a cab and went back to the bar. Several of the group from the ship were still at the bar, some had left.

The four of them had one more round of drinks; then they decided to go out to eat. The women took Dan and Chris down the street to a small restaurant.

They looked at the menus, which were in Korean. It didn't matter, when the waiter came over, Helen and Brenda ordered several items for all of them, and Dan ordered beers all around. They were talking and laughing when the drinks and food arrived.

As with most Korean meals, many small bowls were provided, each with rice, meats and vegetables, flavored with Kimchi, a spicy hot cabbage, sesame oil, chili pepper paste, garlic, ginger and scallions. The food was tongue-numbing, but really good. They ate with steel chop sticks. Although the beers were wet, and helped to quench the hot food, the taste of it left something to be desired. Unfortunately, Dan realized, this beer was not going to be one of his favorites here in the Far East.

It was getting late. They had to be somewhere inside before midnight.

Dan and Chris did not have to be back on the ship until 8:00 a.m. the day after tomorrow – this was a 48-hour liberty. They were in a two-section watch, and weren't scheduled to be on duty until that second day.

Once back on the ship, they would then be required to start their rotation of standing cold-iron watches and working on various repairs, until the boilers would be fired up again, the generators and main engines re-started, shore services secured, and the ship would get underway, back to the gun line. But that was way later.

Helen said, "We need to go home."

"Sounds like a plan," Dan answered. "Lead the way."

Dan and Chris split the bill. Helen took Dan's hand as they left the restaurant, with Brenda and Chris right behind them. They walked up the street to the next block and turned into an alley between two buildings, which led to a set of stairs. The four of them walked up to the second floor and through a doorway to inside the building. It was dimly-lit by one ceiling-mounted bulb in the hallway.

Helen stopped at a door on the right. Brenda took Chris to the next door.

Chris said, "Dan, I'll see you in the morning, buds. We'll grab breakfast."

"Okay, man, take it easy. I'll see you later."

Helen and Brenda took out their keys and the four of them entered their respective rooms. Helen turned on an overhead light.

The room was just slightly larger than a single bed, with a small table next to it containing a wind-up alarm clock, a shelf with four books, a two-drawer cabinet, and a window with a curtain.

Helen locked the door. "Why don't you sit down," she said. Dan sat on the bed. She sat next to him and they kissed each other.

The rest of the night provided Dan with just what he needed, and he returned the favor to Helen. Like in all meaningful human relationships, what matters most is bonding, having that connection, regardless of external factors.

The alarm clock rang loudly the next morning. It was 8:30 a.m. They climbed out of bed. Before doing anything else, Dan said, "I want to give you some spending money for today, since we had such a nice time yesterday and last night."

He handed her ₩ 6,000, about $15.00, an amount that was customary for a day and evening's worth of entertainment with a bar girl in this town, as he had been informed by Chris and some of the other sailors.

He still had about ₩ 10,000 left, about $25.00, plus his spare $10.00.

Helen smiled and said, "That's nice, you still like me. Thanks!" She put the money in her handbag.

Helen then took Dan down the hall to the toilet. She knocked on Brenda's door as she passed by.

"Yeah, I'm there," Chris sounded off.

Dan used the bathroom, brushed his teeth by scrubbing them with a wet finger and combed his hair. He wished he could shave, but it would have to wait. Coming back to the room, he found Helen and gently kissed her before he finished dressing.

"You're not going back to the ship today, so, what should we do?" Helen asked him.

"Well, for starters, how about we have breakfast somewhere?"

"Ooh, I like that," she purred.

"Okay, I'm sure that will be fine for Chris and Brenda."

"Let's find out," Helen said.

They left the room and walked down the hall. Chris and Brenda were just coming out into the hallway.

"Hey, buddy, how's it going," Dan said to Chris.

"I'm good," Chris answered. "Brenda and I got along real good, didn't we sweetheart?"

"Yeah, I'm in love," she said. No mistake, she had said this plenty of times before, but it was a good-natured delivery.

"How are you and Helen doing?" Chris asked.

"Just fine," as he smiled at her. "We're coming back here tonight, right?"

"Okay with me," Chris said. "That's what we're doing, right, Brenda?"

"I'm with you, Chris," Brenda said.

"Right now, let's get some breakfast," Chris said.

"Great, let's go," Dan said.

They walked down the stairs, out of the alley, down the block and back to the restaurant that they had been to the night before.

Brenda and Helen figured out something to order for their meal. Breakfast included seaweed soup, boiled meat dumplings, some fish, rice, scallions, tea and coffee.

Breakfast over, Dan paid the check and they walked into the street. Helen said, "Do you want to visit the United Nations Memorial Park?" Dan then asked Chris, "What do you say, do you want to start with that?" Chris said to Brenda, "How about you, is that okay?"

"Sure, we should show that to you guys," she said.

They walked to the corner and got into a cab. Helen told the driver where they wanted to go and they drove off.

Arriving at the Memorial, they walked through this martyrs' cemetery that contained the graves of over 2,000 soldiers from sixteen countries that had participated in the Korean War.

They saw the first U.S. flag that was flown in South Korea and the original letter of Armistice that had been sent to the United Nations Secretary General. They spent about an hour touring the fields. They didn't talk much; they just walked slowly through the memorial.

When they finished their walk, Helen suggested that they visit the Beomeosa Buddhist temple containing some of the oldest cultural relics of Korea. They hailed a cab and traveled to this temple.

Arriving there and ascending many steps through several gates, the feeling of serenity, peace, and spirituality affected all of them. Helen and Brenda had been here before, and they pointed out many sites to their boyfriends. It was an informative, relaxing visit. From here, they hailed another cab and rode to the outskirts of the city to Yongungsa Temple. Here they saw an ancient temple composed of huge statues carved into, and built on a spot of the rocky coast facing the Sea of Japan, or the East Sea as the Koreans called it.

They visited one more place, the Pusan Tower. This contained an observatory at the top of the building, about thirty stories up from the surrounding park. There were spectacular views of the city.

By this time it was late in the day and time to eat. They made their way back to the bar neighborhood, but this time they went to a different restaurant. The menu was about the same, offering rice, vegetables, kimchi, and beer.

They finished their meal and headed back to the "Lucky Bar." It was time for a few more drinks, and for dancing, to contemporary American rock music playing on the jukebox. Helen and Dan held hands and talked about topical subjects of culture, and politics as well as family, work and hope.

Since it was getting late, the evening's festivities ended back at Helen's and Brenda's rooms. Once there, Brenda and Chris disappeared into her room.

Before entering the room, Helen said to Dan, "I need to go somewhere for a little while. You go in and I'll be back." She unlocked the door and Dan went inside.

He didn't question her about where she was going or what she was doing. Maybe she was going to see her daughter, maybe she was going to do something else.

It really wasn't his business. She would either be back before curfew, or she wouldn't. He entered her room, turned on the light and sat on the bed. While he waited for her to re-join him, he picked up one of the books on the shelf. It was a Korean comic book. It was written entirely in Korean.

He tried to interpret the action as best as he could simply from the pictures, but it was a bit vague trying to fathom just what it was that he was seeing in this book. The other books, one of which was another graphic novel or comic, were written completely in Korean, and impossible for Dan to read.

An hour went by, then another. While he waited he picked up the comic books several times, flipping through the pages but was just as frustrated. It had been such a wonderful day, why wasn't she here now? He couldn't fathom bursting in on Chris and Brenda as he was sure they were busy with themselves by this time.

As he looked at the clock again Helen came into the room. "Okay, I'm back," she said. "You okay, Dan?"

"I'm fine, now that you're here. Hope everything's alright with you?"

"Sure, no problem," she answered evenly. He didn't ask anything more.

"Helen, let me give you some money for the really great day we had." He gave her the equivalent of $20.00. It wasn't awkward, just business, but Dan was feeling more than just mechanical towards her. Their time together, that to this point was extremely brief, was a personal relationship, with personal communication, more than just business.

"Thanks, Dan. You are a nice guy. I had a nice time today."

"Yeah, me too," he said.

Helen came closer to him and sat on the bed. "I hope you will be safe when you go back to the ship," she said.

"I'll be alright," he said. "I'm used to it."

"Yes," Helen said, "But there's the war."

"Well, mostly we're not too close to the fighting so I should be okay. Don't worry about me. But I'm worried about you, taking care of your daughter, and working."

"It's not so bad. I make money. I see her, and my mother, and I meet nice guys," she said.

Certainly Dan was just one of many men that she had meetings with over the years, but this time they seemed to have meant something more to each other, and were well intentioned in how special this time had been to them.

This might not have been the most important relationship that he and she had ever had, but it did have levels of intellectual depth and elevated emotions. For Dan, it had been a short, intense, and vital liaison.

With the war in the background and with her responsibilities, there were many uncertainties, but at least they had these brief moments for themselves.

Gently he started to remove her clothing while removing his. They spent the night together in that room, caressing and exploring. This second night was to be his last with Helen. He was due back to the ship with Chris the next morning for second section watch.

They woke up early to the alarm clock. Dan and Chris had to be back by 0700.

Helen and Dan got dressed, left the room, took care of personal business and then met Chris and Brenda in the hall.

The four of them walked down the stairs to the street, then to the corner where they found a cab.

Kissing each other and saying goodbye, they parted, Dan and Chris to the war, Helen and Brenda to find someone else for the next evening. It was a timeless encounter.

It was a short ride back to the pier. Dan and Chris didn't talk much about anything. They were tired and satisfied. Dan was pensive and would hold the memory of this port visit for a long time. He said to Chris, "That was a special time for me, man. I think I fell in love."

"Maybe you did my friend, but you know this can happen a lot in these towns. You take care of yourself keeping these urges in check or you'll be submitting a chit to get approval for a wife to take back to the States."

"Well, I don't know if I'm going that route. But I may see her again next time we're here."

"Okay, have at it, but just try to maintain yourself."

"Don't worry, I got it."

After crossing the ship's brow and going below to their division compartments, they changed into their dungaree working uniforms, had breakfast on the mess deck, formed up for quarters, relieved the watch for those men to now go on liberty, and went to work, through that day and the next.

Getting underway two days later, leaving Pusan, the ship steamed back to the gun line since the crew's primary mission was fighting.

That's the way it went. From here to there and back again, working with the expectation of a spectacular, though short encounter with someone special at next liberty call.

Olongapo City

The main five-inch gun that was mounted on the forecastle of the destroyer that Warren Statler was serving in had been firing onto the beach all night, for the third night running. The ship was in the Gulf of Tonkin, on Yankee Station, just shy of the demilitarized zone separating North and South Vietnam, roughly due east of the city of Da Nang, providing naval gunfire support for in-country troop activities. The war had been going on with United States involvement since before 1964 and wouldn't end until the evacuation of Saigon in 1975. It was now 1973.

Warren was standing watch as an E-4 Boiler Tender Petty Officer Third Class, on the upper level of the forward fire room, monitoring the water level in 1A boiler, supplying steam to the main engines and generators in Main Control and the after engine room. It was 140° F on the upper level in front of that steam drum. He had been on board for eighteen months and was due for rotation to another ship, or to another duty station, in six months. He had been in the Navy for two years and was still on his first enlistment.

The ship had been steaming in the Gulf for seventy-six days straight, firing on the beach or chasing aircraft carriers, to rescue fighter jet pilots who didn't make it back to their ship.

This was a lengthier time at sea than their usual underway deployment of four to five weeks. Being at sea for more than two months was long enough, and the officers and crew on this destroyer were hot, tired and thinking about their next location for liberty.

Although these blue-water sailors had it extraordinarily better at sea than the grunts on the ground, or even the brown-water sailors who were patrolling the coast and rivers of Vietnam, it could be hazardous when the ship got too close to the beach, since the Vietcong's ordinance could reach them.

It went without saying, there was no comparison by any stretch of the imagination that the blue-water sailors had it better to any immeasurable degree than those poor soldiers and Marines on the ground that were in complete misery and indescribable danger. A lot of people were being maimed and killed. It was war.

Some of the work required during gunfire support was to re-arm, that is, to re-stock ordinance, about two or three times per week, depending on how many rounds were being fired. Re-arming would be accomplished at underway replenishment, from an ammunition ship running alongside the destroyer. Underway replenishment is one of the most dangerous operations that two ships can perform. Each vessel must maintain a constant matching speed of about 15 knots (about 24 miles per hour) and needed to sustain a constant distance between them (about 100 feet), with the waves churning against them both, and at night.

Except for a few low-level red lights located at strategic places along the weather decks, it was dark out there.

The ammunition that was being used was the 74-lb. projectiles that of course the sailors called "bullets." These shells also needed 47-lb powder charges in order to fire them.

Every sailor of rate 2nd Class / E-5 and below had to carry both of these items one at a time to the forward ammunition magazine, while cradling each of them like a baby, without holding onto handrails. A sailor could get stuck with having to carry maybe three or four of each of these items every time that underway replenishment was conducted.

After the ordinance was carried to the forward magazine, and was handed off to the Gunners Mates, it was these sailors who were then responsible to lower these munitions into that space, just below the main gun itself.

From what Warren had heard from the Gunners Mates and by how these guys looked, it was no joke about how hot it was in there. This was the Boiler Tender's kinship with the Gunners Mates – a dubious distinction at best. Everyone had their challenges.

Warren fared reasonably well in the heat of the fire room. He was thin, at a height of 5'-6", with short brown hair, matching brown eyes and presented himself with a cheerful, clean-shaven face. His work dungarees were usually as clean as could be expected.

Although he worked in this environment that could be destructive to his clothing, he always ensured that he would never be stopped from going on the beach because he needed a haircut, or was otherwise not squared away.

He had even fought for his fellow BTs to have permission to wear white cotton sox in the heat of the fire room instead of conforming to the requirement of having to wear black sox only as a part of the working uniform of the day. This was a welcome change for these sailors.

During respites from firing the gun or chasing air craft carriers, the ship's crew had pulled liberty in Taiwan, Korea and the Philippines. After this current operation, they were headed back to the Philippines, to Olongapo City in Subic Bay. This was none too soon for the enlisted crew and for the commissioned officers. This was a full-service facility, and they would be able to shut down the engineering plant to make some needed repairs, as well as take advantage of some liberty.

The Philippine islands had jungles and mountains; the country was very lush and primitive. It had museums, parks, and office buildings; it was very civilized.

It was in Subic Bay where the huge military installation, the largest Navy base in the Western Pacific at the time, was located. The wide-open town of Olongapo City was located just outside of the Navy base.

The ship was relieved on Yankee Station by another destroyer and was now in transit to Subic Bay. After a short sail, the ship arrived in Subic and tied up to a pier.

The first thing that the "B" Division sailors did was to refuel the ship. This evolution of taking on oil lasted several hours, since they had not refueled at sea prior to coming into port and they needed almost 100,000 gallons.

Most of the rest of the ship's company from all of the other divisions that didn't have the duty hit the beach for liberty while "B" Division took on fuel.

Warren was used to this, with most of the other non-rated men of his division. Either at sea, when re-fueling took precedence over eating chow, or more important than sleeping, or taking on fuel while tied up at a pier, it also took precedence over "B" Division immediately leaving the ship. Warren's responsibility during these evolutions was to monitor selected fuel tank levels as thousands of gallons of oil were pumped into them.

Once the tanks were topped off and re-fueling was completed, the "B" Division sailors that did not have the watch could get cleaned up and head into town. The watch was either for "cold iron," that is, with most of the physical plant shut down, or for auxiliary steaming, when the boilers would still be firing to make steam for the electrical generators and other selected equipment, but not for the main engines.

Warren, and Ted, another 3rd Class Petty Officer, with Ricky and Thomas, two E-3 Firemen, and Dave, a 2nd Class Electrician, got cleaned up, changed into their civilian clothes and went topside to the Quarterdeck to leave the ship, since they did not have any watches to stand until the next day.

They were in a two-section watch group and could spend the rest of this day and that night on liberty, then would catch a day's work the next day starting at 0800 following quarters. Then they would leave Subic Bay after that.

Saluting the Officer of the Deck at the gangway, each one of them stated, "Request permission to leave the ship, sir."

"Permission granted," the OOD saluted back, and each one of them stepped onto the gangway, saluted the American flag at the stern, and crossed the brow onto the pier. The old days of presenting a Liberty Pass to leave the ship had been replaced by the freedom to perform this ritual of seeking permission to cross the brow onto the beach while wearing civilian clothes, if one didn't have the watch or weren't serving restricted duty. As long as one had dog tags hanging around one's neck and had a military ID card, which was as good as a Passport, a sailor could leave the ship.

Walking away from the end of the pier, they had to cross a bridge over what tried to pass for a small river, to get to the main gate of the military base that led out through to Olongapo City. Of course, they had been warned that to fall into this body of water could mean almost certain death because of the pollution level.

They weren't kidding. It did look like you could just about walk across the water to get to the other side.

Not much different from the infamous Gowanus Canal back in Brooklyn, New York, where Warren had come from before joining the Navy.

That body of water in his home town, however, had a perpetual film of oil and other choice matter floating on top of it for many years before it had been cleaned up.

Or it was like the canal in Venice that the actress Katharine Hepburn insisted to fall into by herself during the shooting of one of her films, rather than use a stunt double. She developed an eye infection that affected her for quite some time afterwards. This little creek in Olongapo appeared to be in about the same condition as both of these.

Here though, there were children in boats who were begging the sailors for coins – a pretty sorry sight. And they would dive right into the water to retrieve any money that was tossed in by the sailors. It looked to Warren and the others that they lived through it – at least the swimmers came up out of the water, so the warning of certain death was obviously exaggerated.

After crossing over the water, they stopped at the Enlisted Men's Club, for rated 3rd Class sailors and below, and converted most of their money into Pesos, at the current exchange rate then of roughly $6.50 Pesos to $1.00 U.S.

They continued into the town, which consisted of bar after bar lining both sides of the main street, a liberty port that could remind one of the wild west of yesteryear in the United States during the 1800s. The streets weren't even paved in Olongapo. Fortunately, for this liberty, the sailors didn't have to wear their dress whites, but could wear civilian clothes; otherwise, their uniforms would have been ruined by the mud.

Like any of the other waterfront locales that Warren had visited as a sailor, this town was all that it was rumored to be. There wasn't much in the way of cultural venues here; it was simply a place to unwind from the rigors of steam sailing and war.

The group stopped in at one of the bars on the main street, the "Two Steps Inn." The sailors placed themselves on stools at the bar. It didn't take long for each of them to be joined by one of the hostesses.

A slight, slim, pretty dark-haired woman wearing black pants and a plain blue blouse approached Warren.

"Can I sit next to you?" she asked shyly.

"By all means, please," Warren answered.

"How are you doing?" she asked him as she sat down.

"I'm good," he said. "How are you?"

"I am very hot in here," she said, but only as a statement. Warren didn't read anything into that. "If you are hot in here too like me, maybe we need some cold drinks," she said

"I got it," Warren said. He pulled out some Pesos that he had exchanged at the Enlisted Club before coming into town and ordered two drinks, a gin and tonic for himself and a lady's drink for her.

"What's your name?" she asked.

"My name's Warren, what's yours?" he asked.

"I am Nellie," she said.

The drinks were set in front of them. He picked his up and she did the same. "Here's to a fun evening," Warren said.

"Sure," she said. "We can have fun."

They drank; then Warren said, "Would you care to dance?"

"I would love to," she said.

He took her hand and they proceeded to the center of the dance floor. Other couples were already there. Contemporary rock music was blaring from the juke box. They danced two fast dances, then they held each other for a slower song. Her head barely reached to the bottom of his nose, and she smelled so good. It had been a while since Warren had been with someone.

He had been working and standing watches for sixteen hour days in the midst of the noise and heat and smoke of an operating warship and was now unwinding into a relaxed happiness of human contact.

After their dance, they walked back to the bar and sat down. They talked about the music that was playing, what music they liked, and that they both liked American country music.

"That was the new Dolly Parton song playing, 'Jolene,' she said.

"That was such a sad song."

"But we don't have to listen to sad songs," Nellie said. "I know a club that plays live country music. Do you want me to take you there?"

"That would be fine with me," Warren said. "Hey, Ted," he called over to him talking to another one of the hostesses, "Nellie and I are leaving to go down the street. I'll see you later or back on the ship."

"Just make sure you're back by 0700 buds," Ted said. "You know we have to be back in the morning."

"Yeah, no problem, man, I'll make it back," he said.

"Come on, Nellie, show me the way," he said.

Nellie took his hand and they left the bar. Walking on the street, they passed several other bars and clubs. They passed a man selling lizards, someone else selling roasted monkey meat, which Warren passed on, and a guy selling butterfly knives.

A previous warning about "butterfly knives" from other sailors who had been in the Far East for a long time made you sit up and take notice.

Most of the women in Olongapo City were supposedly packing these approximately six inch long, double bladed knives, which they pulled out from some secret, hidden spot, for which the business end was quickly exposed by flipping the handle around in a swift, practiced move.

They were called butterfly knives not just because of their operation and shape but more because to "butterfly" meant that you were going out with one woman while two-timing her by seeing someone else.

This was a very exciting though very foolhardy thing for a sailor to do. The women in Olongapo were notorious for having no sense of humor about this sort of thing and were quick to respond by using their secret weapon. The sailors had all heard stories of men being hurt badly by a jealous girlfriend.

These were very beautiful, very dangerous pieces of hardware being handled by some very beautiful, very dangerous women. Fortunately, Nellie seemed to Warren to be a nice person.

They proceeded together past these vendors to the club where Nellie was taking Warren. Nellie could not have entered this club unless she was escorted by one of the sailors, as it was required for everyone of the bar girls. They needed an escort to go from club to club. It was just one of the rules. There was another rule - a curfew, from midnight until 7:00 a.m.

Martial Law was in effect at the time under President Ferdinand Marcos where the Army was the police force and everyone had to be off the streets – either home with someone or back through the main gate of the base on their way to a ship.

Walking into the club that Nellie had taken him to, and finding a table near the stage, which was set up with band instruments, they joined other sailors, and their girlfriends just in time for the show.

A waiter came over to their table. "Let me have a San Miguel and anything the lady wants," Warren said. San Miguel was the great Philippine beer that Warren was drinking and that he would continue to drink for years afterward, whenever he could get it.

The waiter came back with their drinks, a beer with a glass for Warren and a house drink for Nellie.

Warren paid the waiter and said, "Mara Ming salamat" which meant thank you very much in Tagalog, the language of the Philippines.

"I am impressed," Nellie said. "I didn't know that you spoke Filipino."

"Well, not really," Warren said. "A basic word or two here and there, like paki-mo."

"That's good," she said, "You know how to say please. I like that. You have respect."

"It's just the very least I can do," Warren said. "We Americans and you Filipinos have such a long and valuable history and friendship. Saying a couple of words in Tagalog isn't much of anything to show respect, but maybe it's something, anyway."

"No, it is a great thing that you do. Be proud of it," she said.

"Thanks," he said.

"How much school do you have?" she asked him.

"I graduated high school, then I took classes at a junior college and got a two-year degree. How about you?" he asked.

"I went to high school, then I started college at a public school in Manila for business administration, but my family didn't have enough money for me to keep going," she said.

"That's too bad," Warren said. "It's tough to keep going to school without money."

"So, that is why I came to work here in Olongapo," Nellie said.

"Oh, do you have family here in Olongapo?" he asked.

"No, not here, but my grandmother, brother, and sister live in Manila," she said.

"Really, do you get to visit them much?" he asked.

"Sometimes," she said. "Mostly I am here. Have you been to Manila?"

"Yes, once, a few months ago," he said. "We're going back there soon." Warren wasn't going to give Nellie the details of when they would be there, that would border on military stupidity, and he didn't even really know exactly when they would be there anyway, but he had heard that they would be pulling liberty there shortly.

"Maybe I will go back to school one of these days."

"That would be great if you could get back to school. You are pretty young. Hopefully you'll get back to it," he said.

"I can try. That's all I can do," she said. "How about you? Are you going to stay in the Navy, or are you going back to school?"

"Well, I don't know right now," he answered. "I'm okay, it's not too bad in the service, but I'll see how I feel two years from now."

"You'll figure it out, like I will," she said.

"I guess we both will," he said.

They left the topic there. Discussing some of their past and future plans was a normal activity for people, even in the midst of this simulated date.

A man stepped onto the stage and announced the name of the group that was going to play, and the show began. This entertainment by a local Philippine band excellently playing contemporary and classic American country music was a quality performance, rivaling anything that one could hear recorded on a major label or could see on the "Ed Sullivan Show," for example, or in any major club in New York or any other city. It was a real treat. The band played several country songs and some couples danced. Nellie and Warren danced together blissfully for one song; then they sat down again to listen.

They ordered some food – a typical plate of stir-fried noodles with pieces of curried chicken and vegetables.

"You like this place?" Nellie asked.

"Nice," he said. "Music is great. This is a really great show, isn't it?" he asked.

"These are very good songs," she said. "Sometimes they make me very sad."

"I'm sorry," Warren said. "But you know how country music is. It could tell a really down story or be really silly. There's always something for everyone."

"Yes, so between country and rock I find something great to listen to," Nellie said.

"That's the same for me," Warren said. "Especially country, but there's also those rock and roll oldies."

"Oh, sure," she said. "I know all of that music. They play that in some of the clubs here in Olongapo, and on the radio. Maybe we could go to one of these clubs later."

"Well, maybe," he said. "Why don't we see how late it is after this club? Maybe we'll have to be home somewhere by that time. Do you have a place nearby where we could stay?" he asked.

"Of course, I think we are going to go home together, yes?" she smiled at him.

"That's just what I was thinking, too," Warren smiled back. "How old are you that you like rock and roll?" Warren asked.

"Me, I am twenty-two. How old are you?" she asked him.

"I'm twenty-four," he told her.

"Well, each of us is not too old or too young," she said.

"Old enough for what?" he said.

"Oh, I don't know, just for life," she said.

"I guess, I just never thought about it much. You are what you are, where you are," Warren said.

"You are right," Nellie said. "It doesn't matter much anyway."

"What matters right now is that we're together and having a good time, right?" he said.

"Yes, you are right," she responded. "Let's enjoy the show."

After the band finished their set, the announcer introduced a group of acrobats who demonstrated superb tumbling and balancing accompanied by an accordion player.

It was fascinating to Warren and seemed so to Nellie, even though Warren thought that she had probably seen these performers many times before.

It was getting late. Nellie said, "We need to go home now, before curfew."

"That's fine," Warren answered. "Take me where we need to go."

They left the club, as did several of the other couples. Warren felt good that he did not have Cinderella Liberty, where he would have had to be back on the ship by mid-night. At least tonight he was able to stay on the beach until quarters the next morning, after acknowledging that he was present, would have to go to work and stand watches. He was looking forward to having a relaxing evening with Nellie, after all of these past days at sea.

Nellie led him farther up the street, until the bars started to thin out, then abruptly ended, where an enclave of small, stucco-covered bungalows were located. They didn't talk very much; they just walked in the damp heat of this tropical night. Nellie brought him to one of the cabins and opened the door with her key. Walking in, Nellie turned on a table lamp near the door and Warren looked around.

It had a sitting room at the entrance which continued to a small kitchen with a slab sink and an LPG gas stove. Beyond that he could see another room, the bedroom. After drinking the several beers, Warren needed the bathroom, and Nellie pointed him in the right direction, next to the bedroom.

He turned on the overhead light and saw that it had a toilet, a large metal barrel full of water with a dipper hanging over the edge, ready for bathing, with the waste water to run into a floor drain in the center of the tiled floor.

Warren came out of the bathroom and found Nellie sitting demurely on the bed. Warren was impressed. They were getting along well and had the same thing on their minds.

For Warren, it was an instinctive liaison mixed with the disguise of romance. For Nellie, it was an occupation varied with the masquerade of a relationship, but not always so, for either one of them.

Sometimes, many times, more than just having the veneer of affection, there was a genuine connection of love when two people met, even in this artificial setting. There was something serious here that Warren felt, even though they had only known each other for a short time, and it seemed to him that Nellie returned the emotion.

It was difficult to accurately judge the sincerity of what they were feeling. The war was on, she was surrounded by poverty, friends, strangers and entertainment. There were only temporary moments of tenderness, understanding and holding on to each other, at this time, and at times with others. Sometimes, they would each be holding on to someone else.

It was hard to sustain the emotions required to be in a meaningful, fulfilling relationship, unless a couple could be with each other for more than just intermittent moments.

As intense or encapsulated as these times may have been for them, their being together in these conditions was so real to them, although synthetic.

They slowly undressed each other. Nellie placed their clothes, including her butterfly knife, on a table next to the bed. He hadn't really thought much that she might have had one, but she did. He didn't believe that she would have any cause to threaten him with it. He did believe that he was in love. They went into the bathroom to shower-bathe on that floor. It was luxurious and refreshing in that heat. Finishing their washing, they retired for the evening.

The alarm clock rang loudly the next morning. They dressed quickly. Warren said, "Nellie, let me leave you with some Pesos for whatever you need or for what you want to do today."

He placed $140.00 Pesos in $20.00 bills on the table, about $20.00 U.S.

"You are very nice, Warren. Thanks," she said. "This will help my family."

"I'll be on the ship today and tonight," he said, "then we'll be getting underway. How about I visit you in Manila when I get there?"

"Wow, you want to get together with me in Manila?" she said. "We can do that. If I know when you will be there, then I could meet you somewhere."

"I'm not sure when we'll be there, but how long would it take you to get to Manila from here?" he asked.

"I could get there in about three hours by bus," she said. "It's about 100 kilometers from here."

"Okay, how about I call you when I get to Manila and then you come there?" he said. "Let me have a telephone number where I can reach you."

Nellie went into the kitchen and pulled a pad and pencil from one of the shelves above the sink. She wrote a phone number on one of the pages and handed it to Warren.

"This is Jennifer's number, my girlfriend. Call her when you know where you are," she said. "I will be with her, or she will get me. We could meet at the Jose Rizal monument in Rizal Park."

"Ah, yes, the national hero of the Philippines," Warren said.

"You know about Jose Rizal?" she asked.

"Yes, I do," he said. "He was a poet and the greatest hero of the Philippines, who worked to gain the country's independence from Spain."

"That is so good that you know that," she said. "We are very proud of Jose Rizal and what he did for the Filipino people."

"That's for sure," he said. "It's a great thing that he did for the country. I don't know a lot about him, but I remember some things from high school when we studied Europe and Colonialism."

"Yes, we learned all about our history in high school, too," she said. "Countries need their independence, and so do the people."

"I agree. Most of the democracies in this world, like the Philippines, were modeled after the United States," he said. "I guess that's why the U.S. and the Philippines are such good friends."

"That's true, our countries, our people, are very good allies," she said. "It has been good for both of us."

"Well, meeting in Manila will continue the friendship, at least for you and me," Warren said. "I will call you sometime soon when I get to Manila and we'll meet up."

"Okay, I hope to hear from you," she said.

"You will," Warren said, with conviction.

They left the cabin and walked towards the bar district.

They walked into town. A Jeepney was parked in front of one of the clubs. This was a completely Filipino vehicle that was half-taxicab, half-jeep, and was vividly decorated with wildly colorful painted patterns and had many bangles and other things hanging from most of the open window frames. They climbed in the back of the Jeepney and Nellie told the driver to take them to the gate at the Navy base down the street.

They reached their destination and Warren jumped off. He handed Nellie enough coins to cover the ride, which cost less than $1.00. He leaned into the cab and they kissed each other goodbye.

Warren walked through the gate, onto the base, past the Enlisted Men's Club, across the bridge, along the pier and onto the gangway to his ship.

He saluted the flag, then, while saluting the Officer of the Deck, he asked permission to come aboard.

He walked along the weather deck to one of the open doors, and went below to the "M" & "B" Division compartment to change into his dungarees, the working uniform of the day.

He gathered in sections on the fantail with the sailors that had gone over together the day before and the rest of the Engineering Department. They listened to the Plan of the Day scan-read by the Main Propulsion Assistant, a Lieutenant Junior Grade (jg) who had the duty this day. Ship's company were at quarters long enough for Colors, that is, for raising the American Flag while they saluted as a group, then they were dismissed to get to work in the spaces below. Warren was completely happy and was looking forward to his visit with Nellie in Manila.

Two days later, the ship got underway, back to the gun line in the Gulf of Tonkin. They spent the next six weeks steaming on station, firing their main gun, plane guarding and conducting anti-submarine warfare monitoring. Then it was time for Manila.

They left the Gulf and traveled for one day to Manila harbor. While waiting to tie up to the pier, they were able to go swimming in the harbor.

While in this section of the ocean, the Gunners Mates were on station in the motor whaleboat, with pieces, that is, with rifles, watching out for sea snakes and other creatures while those sailors that chose to enjoyed their swim.

At one point someone yelled out that there was a dead baby floating by – it seemed to be just a sea story since the ship did not make any effort to conduct a rescue or recovery.

Since they had refueled while underway before entering the harbor, Warren and the rest of "B" Division did not have to take on oil when they arrived at the pier. Finishing breakfast, Warren left the ship with several of the other Boiler Tenders. Once Warren was set up, the group would be taking a cab into the city and would go their separate ways. It was 8:30 a.m. Warren and the other sailors that he was with had forty-eight hour liberty, providing two overnights. He found a pay phone at the end of the pier, and called Nellie's friend.

Surprisingly, Nellie answered the phone. "Hello, Warren. I am so happy you called. I was a lonely girl waiting for you," which sounded sincere. Did Warren believe such a statement? He wanted to, but only almost did. This visit with her in Manila would reveal how they really felt about each other, he thought.

"Me too, honey," Warren said anyway.

"I'm leaving now and will meet you at Jose Rizal's statue in a few hours," she said.

"Okay," he said. "When you get here we'll have lunch."

"I can't wait," Nellie said. "I'll be there soon."

Warren and the rest of the liberty party climbed into two of the several Jeepneys waiting at the pier, and told the driver to take them to the center of Manila, to a restaurant that one of them knew.

Entering the place, they were really looking for a nice breakfast. Although Navy chow was good, it would be a treat to have a restaurant meal.

They finished their breakfast of tortas with longganisas, that is, omelets with sausages, then left the restaurant to walk around the city.

Although Warren knew where he needed to go, the rest of them had no particular agenda, except to hit any number of the bars and clubs in town a little later in the day to meet women.

It was getting closer to noon and Warren bid the group goodbye, then jumped into a passing Jeepney. He told the driver to take him to the statue of Jose Rizal, which he did. Warren placed himself near the statue in the park and maintained a visual search for Nellie in all directions. It could take her four hours to travel by bus from Olongapo to Manila, or it could take her longer. Warren did not have to wait, however. Nellie was approaching him after he had been there about an hour.

Nellie came up to him. "So good to see you. Now I am happy again."

"What a nice thing to say," Warren said. "I'm glad you're here."

They kissed each other, for a long moment. This meeting was actually happening, as complicated as it was to make it happen. It was going to be a good meeting. Warren did feel good.

They walked through the park, holding hands. They bought lunch of fried lumpia, a type of spring roll with plantain, and some fish balls from a food vendor. They sat at a nearby table.

"It is so nice here," Warren said.

"It is, isn't it?" Nellie said. "I have been to Rizal Park many times. It's nice that we have this in the middle of the city. It's like having Central Park in New York, but of course not so big."

"I've been to Central Park a few times," Warren said. "My family is from the Bronx, but I was in New York for my Navy induction ceremony. Never did get to Central Park much though."

"Well, maybe someday you will get there more."

"Oh, I don't know, maybe."

"So, how about we visit the Jose Rizal Museum," she asked him.

"Absolutely, I would like to see that."

They left the lunch area and climbed into a Jeepney at the edge of the park.

They visited the museum devoted to the poet Jose Rizal, the greatest national hero of the Philippines, who worked to gain the country's independence from Spain.

The museum had re-created the cell in which he was imprisoned for his efforts. Warren felt privileged and humbled to have been able to visit this place.

"Why don't we go to visit my family here in Manila?" Nellie asked.

"Sure," Warren said, "That would be an honor."

They walked to a Jeepney and rode it to where Nellie told the driver, somewhere in the middle of the city. Warren paid the fare when they arrived.

She took him into a small alley leading from the main street, to an inner unpaved courtyard, walking through a small flock of chickens pecking around their feet, to the front door.

They walked through the door into the kitchen, where several people were sitting at the table in the center of the room.

Nellie said, "This is Warren who is visiting me today."

Warren said, "Very pleased to meet everyone."

Her grandmother and other assorted relatives were in the room. He was invited to sit down at the table and have lunch.

The grandmother served white rice in wooden bowls. They used their fingers. Warren couldn't help noticing that there were several very small, very live ants also sharing these bowls.

He could just barely concentrate on the ants, however, as he also watched the very live lizards crawling on the walls.

No one else mentioned any of the critters sharing in their meal, so he and the others just kept on with the light conversation discussing where he was from in the United States, that he was of German descent, that he had spent the past two years in the Navy, and that he and Nellie had visited the museum. He was a good guest.

The family didn't seem to have any doubt about, or to openly mind that their granddaughter was earning her living as a bar girl in Olongapo, one of the most notorious and dangerous places in the Far East. Everybody has to make a living. It was just part of the culture in that place in that time of the war.

They finished their meal and chatted a little while longer. Soon, they were ready to leave.

Warren was grateful for the meal, its condiments notwithstanding, but this was more of an experience meeting Nellie's family and sharing a meal than any of his buddies would probably have in Manila. He needed cigarettes and bought a pack of Camels from a vendor. Here, he thought he could get his brand. Not exactly, however. These were some kind of Camel-authorized, home-grown variety.

The packaging was almost the same but the taste was way off, more vegetable-like than tasting like tobacco. This didn't stop him from smoking them, though.

Nellie told Warren that she had arranged to have them stay at a house of a friend of hers out of the city somewhere in the jungle, in one of the rural barangays, or small towns.

They took a bus out of Manila, for a long ride on a road that became more desolate as they traveled farther and farther outside of the city. Warren had no idea where they were going, but he knew that he was in caring hands.

By this time, however, although they seemed to have established a meaningful friendship, Warren couldn't help knowing that for him, it was destined to end totally and forever in a very short time. This was just the nature of these relationships, regardless if they were electrifying in their emotional power, they were for most of the participants so temporary.

After two hours of riding, they were let out at a crossroads and walked right into a town of wood huts that were built on either side of a main road. Several adults and children were standing in the road, and other people were sitting in front of some of the huts.

Nellie walked up to the group of people in the road and introduced Warren as her friend from the United States. Some of these people were her friends; some were her relatives. Warren was polite and friendly; he was going to be a good guest just like he had been in Manila. Most everyone was speaking English, with others speaking Tagalog.

They were invited to walk over to the house that they were going to stay in for the night, which they were going to have for themselves. It was a one room shack, furnished with two chairs, a small table and a bed. There was no electricity, just an oil lamp on the table. The bathroom was not in the hut, but there was an outhouse a little ways at the back of it.

Nellie brought Warren outside to some semblance of a barbecue pit, with several carcasses already roasting on spits, with some of the townsfolk that he had already met, standing and sitting around a large table. It was time to eat. Warren didn't need to guess what they were having for dinner.

One of the carcasses had been poor Fido just a short time before, the others similar breeds, that is known in the Philippines as Asocena, dog meat. Although eaten legally in those days, in these current times dog meat has been outlawed except for ceremonial meals.

Oh, well, thought Warren, although he had passed on the monkey meat back in Olongapo, when in Rome . . .

Actually, to Warren, it was not too far off the mark; the Asocena tasted somewhat like chicken, though with more fat.

Everyone else was happy chowing down on tonight's obviously standard fare, enjoying the food with bottles of San Miguel.

The meal came to a close and they said goodnight to everyone, Warren thanking them for their hospitality. They went into the shack and lit the lamp. They were tired from the day's travels, especially Nellie, and the lamp did not stay lit for very long.

Lowering the wick until it was extinguished, they climbed into bed, skipping a shower-bath, then enjoyed each other until they fell asleep.

The next morning, while getting dressed, Warren said, "Nellie, I want to give you some money for your family." He handed her $350.00 in Pesos, about $60.00 U.S. It was a reasonable amount, if you could place a price on what they had shared, back in Olongapo, Manila and here in this town.

It was early in the morning. It was quiet in the town. They left the hut and walked to the main road.

They waited at the crossroads for about a half hour until the bus stopped to pick them up for the long ride back to Manila. They mostly cuddled and slept on the bus.

As they approached the city, Warren said, "I had a wonderful couple of days, Nellie. I'm not going to forget how nice a time we had together."

"I am very happy that we spent these days with each other," Nellie said. "I enjoyed being with you and taking you to places." She always spoke so politely – after all, she had been to college.

"Yeah, too bad we have to say goodbye," he said.

"Me too," she said, "It was so very nice."

They got off the bus near the waterfront, where Warren could get a Jeepney to the pier. They kissed each other for a long time; then said their final goodbyes.

Leaving the Philippines this time and this sweet person was sad but inevitable for Warren. As close as he thought they were to each other, and it was so easy to fall in love here, it wasn't realistic that he, or she, could keep this relationship going.

A sailor 10,000 miles from home in a foreign port, in love with a bar hostess, a prostitute - maybe that could work in books, or in movies, but most likely not often in the real world. For Warren, it was back to the gun line in the Gulf of Tonkin; for Nellie, it was back to the bar in Olongapo City.

Tattoo

Coming off the gun line during the war in Vietnam, one of the ports that sailors traveled to for "R & R," that is, Rest & Recreation, was Hong Kong, the Pearl of the Orient, the bustling, cross-roads city of the world.

Gordon Sikes had been serving on an old, well-worn destroyer in the main engine room as an E-6 / 1st Class Petty Officer Machinist Mate, supervising men who ran the throttles, the electric generators, and the fresh water distillation plant. During this particular period of providing shore gunfire support and plane guarding, the ship had been underway for seven weeks and they were scheduled to be in Hong Kong for five days. Based on their watch sections, Gordon would be on the beach for three of those five days. It was September, 1972.

R & R is a respite greater than standard liberty that is designed to refresh military personnel, away from the combat zone. Some went on R & R in Singapore or elsewhere, but this ship was going to Hong Kong. The ship anchored in the harbor with one other U.S. Naval ship, a ship of the Canadian Navy, and other merchant ships.

About six sailors at a time would climb down the accommodation ladder, basically similar to a flight of stairs, which had been rigged onto the side of their ship.

They would step into small boats powered by a hand paddle mounted at the stern. These boats were operated by locals who would take the sailors to the Fenwick Pier landing near the China Fleet Club. This was a mall-type department store that catered to sailors and tourists.

Amongst many things, one significant quality about the harbor as noticed by Gordon was its unmistakable smell. An overpowering aroma resembling what he could best describe as a mixture of fuel oil, peanut oil, rotten fish and the teeming humanity of the living quarters on the Sampans and Junks jammed in the water. As Gordon found out, Sampans are for living on and Junks are for transporting cargo. The harbor was filled with these vessels.

Although Gordon had been in the Navy for eight years, this was his first time in Hong Kong. He had recently transferred to this ship from his previous attachment to a fleet oiler in the Atlantic. As a career-minded Petty Officer making rate, he was seeking to expand his travel experiences and technical expertise. He knew that requesting a Pacific billet would in all likelihood result in serving time on a warship in the Gulf of Tonkin, but he was secure in the knowledge that he could make a positive impact on his divisional duties in the engineering spaces as well as enhance his personal experience in the exotic Far East.

Gordon was twenty-seven years old, never married, standing 5'-10" and well-built. His dark brown hair was worn quite short in strict military compliance, which complemented his clean-shaven face with brown, steady eyes. He was confident, a good leader, trained in personnel management and had a plan to make the service a career. His past civilian life had included working as an auto mechanic in Philadelphia.

On this first day in Hong Kong, Gordon went over with several other Machinist Mates and Boiler Tenders, and with his closest buddy, Aaron Thompson, an E-5 / 2nd Class Petty Officer who worked with Gordon on various watches. As they stepped into the liberty boat, Gordon looked at the skyline of thoughrally modern office buildings and apartment houses along the edge of the city and called out to Aaron, "Check out the scene – what a sight!"

"Wait until you see the rest of the place," Aaron said. He also hailed from a northeastern city, Hartford, Connecticut. "It is screaming with life," he went on. "This is one of the most overcrowded cities in the world. These people are crammed into every inch of the place, even the roof-tops."

"Yeah, we were warned about them," Gordon said. "Strictly unauthorized places to be. As much as I'd like to check them out, seems like a guy could get killed up there; it's a little too dark and sinister. I think I'll skip it."

"And best we should," Aaron said. "I've only been to Hong Kong once before and while I wanted to go up there, it just didn't seem worth it to take my life in my hands to do so. Later for that."

The boat landed them at the pier. Gordon, Aaron, and the others were headed first to the club to exchange currency. At the current rate then of approximately $5.60 US to $10.00 HK, their money was going to stretch. Many items, especially clothes, were very inexpensive. Hong Kong was well-known for producing quality custom-tailored clothing at bargain prices. Stepping into the shopping facility, they exchanged money, then did some window-shopping.

One of the guys couldn't resist and was measured for a set of dress blues made to order out of gabardine. This was a fitted uniform made out of very wearable material that was much more comfortable than the Navy-issue 100% wool outfits, which included a thirteen-button pair of pants and a white-piped jumper.

Two other men selected "Liberty Cuffs," which they would later sew into the sleeves of their dress blue jumpers. These were decorative patches placed on the insides of the jumper sleeve ends so that when the cuffs were turned up to keep the white piping clean, especially at a bar, these patches would show beautiful dragons or other designs instead of the plain interior wool. By this, however, the authorized liberty outfit for enlisted sailors was civilian clothes, rather than a dress blue or dress white uniform, and Liberty Cuffs were no longer really necessary.

Gordon did not feel the need to embellish his dress uniform, nor to replace it with gabardine, to basically just wear it for transit between duty stations or for full-dress ceremonies – he would stick with his Navy-issue wool.

Since they had all discussed that they would devote the first day to sight-seeing, with the evening for pursuing drinks and female companionship, they decided to take the peak tram, a cable-hauled funicular railway, up the mountainside to the top of Victoria Peak to see all of the harbor below.

When in the Atlantic fleet, Gordon had been to Puerto Rico, and into the Mediterranean, to Naples, Barcelona, Athens and other ports, but the view from Victoria Peak overlooking the city of Hong Kong and the harbor below was completely breathtaking. They could see the harbor filled with ships of all types, colors, and vintages that were flying flags from an array of countries. The shore line surrounding the harbor was framed by towering skyscrapers of classic and ultra-modern architectural styles, with those providing the foreground to a backdrop of mountains.

Taking the train back down, they walked through the city, exploring the shops and street life. The group decided to have lunch. Stopping into a cubbyhole of a restaurant along a busy street, they seated themselves and looked over the menus, which were written in Chinese and English.

They each ordered soup, and cold beers. After placing the order, Gordon and Josh, another machinist, both noticed at the same time through a doorway what was in the back room of the establishment

Cooing softly were live pigeons in cages stacked against the walls.

"This meal is going to be a big reality check," Gordon said.

Aaron said, "Yeah, there's lots of things in this town you've never had before."

"Well, I'm hungry, so let's have at it," said Gordon.

When the bowls were placed on the table in front of them, they took one look at the soup which was looking right back at them.

Floating there amongst the vegetables were items that appeared to be eyeballs from some unknown origin. These sailors didn't miss a beat – they were there for the duration. They all looked at each other, looked at the soup looking back at them, shared a nervous laugh and dug in. In spite of the unusual assortment of ingredients, with the main focus in these bowls tasting somewhat like mushrooms, they seemed to enjoy the lunch

Leaving the restaurant, they traveled by trolley to Tiger Balm Gardens, since demolished; at the time, however, the Garden was a delightful inner sanctum located within the boundaries of a private residence, which included open-air dioramas depicting frightening scenes of classic Chinese mythology.

By this time in the early evening, they were ready for dinner. They chose to eat at the Four Seasons Restaurant. Just like the same fabulous establishment located in New York City, this partner place featured friendly waiters wearing tuxedos providing impeccable service.

Each one of the group really splurged on this meal, ordering filet mignon with all the trimmings, and having flaming cherries jubilee for desert. The meal was very expensive, but no matter, they were essentially on vacation.

Now, full of food, they needed to find some female companionship for the evening. They headed by cab to the famed Wanchai, or Suzy Wong district, backdrop for the 1960 movie, "The World of Suzy Wong," starring the superb actor William Holden and the well-known Chinese actress Nancy Kwan.

In the film, he's a struggling artist from the United States in post World War II Hong Kong, and she's a struggling bar girl. He is living in a cheap hotel where the proprietor is shocked that a guest would want to rent a room by the month and not by the hour here in the Wanchai district. In amongst the bars and clubs, they meet and fall in love. There are other issues concerning her child, racism and tragedy – it is a poignant story.

Gordon was quite familiar with the movie and was absolutely in awe to be here in this remarkable place. He was prepared for adventure when he walked into the first club that the group entered.

He stepped up to the bar with Aaron to order a drink and immediately a glamorous looking, well-dressed woman with black hair, standing only as tall as Gordon's shoulders, slid in beside him, and a similarly-dressed woman was suddenly standing next to Aaron.

"Hello, sailor, how are you?" she asked Gordon.

"I'm doing just fine, honey, how are you?"

"I would be much better if I could have a drink," she answered. She was well-spoken, although with an accent. Many people outside of the United States are at least bi-lingual with English as their other language.

"I'll take care of that." He signaled the bartender and a drink appeared in front of her. They lifted their glasses and Gordon said, "Here's to you, honey – what's your name?" He almost knew what was coming – after all, this was Wanchai.

"I am Nancy Kwan," she smiled.

This statement of identification was very common. Many of the women in the bars responded with this actress' name. They were very familiar with this famous actress and certainly liked to mischievously tease bright-eyed, hopeful sailors.

"Who are you?" she asked.

"Me? I'm William Holden."

She stared at him for a moment, then she laughed out loud. Gordon guessed that she didn't expect someone to know Nancy's counterpart from the movie – most people probably didn't unless they were movie fans.

"That's a good one. No, really, what is your name?" she asked.

"I'm Gordon," he told her. "And you, what's your name?"

"I am really Kim," she answered. Then she asked him, "Oh, but you know the story?"

"Yes, I know, like we're here in the world of Suzy Wong," he said. "Seems like you know the movie, too, right?"

"Yes, I know, I have seen it, a long time ago."

"Are you an actress?" he asked her.

She smiled, "No, I am too young and too busy working to be a movie star."

"I can appreciate that," he said. "It must be difficult, but you know, I am looking for a nice working girl tonight."

After a long day of sightseeing and eating, Gordon didn't need to spend a long evening courting someone at the bar. He was here for two overnights of R & R liberty and would just as soon call it a night.

"I understand," she said. "Maybe you can take me home." She was being just as direct as Gordon.

"Okay, Kim, how about we dance for a little while and then maybe we go somewhere private?" He was being pretty blunt, but didn't want to waste much time. The evening was young, but it was getting old fast. Before leaving the bar after a short while of dancing, he tapped Aaron on the shoulder to say goodnight.

It looked like Aaron was making good time with his new girlfriend, whom he introduced as Joanne.

"Hey, buddy, I will see you in the morning, how about right here in this bar?" Aaron asked.

"Works for me," Gordon said.

Kim and he left the bar and she led him through a narrow alley to a doorway leading up a set of stairs to her room.

She said clinically, "Before we get started any more, I need $100.00."

This was a substantial amount of money, worth at least $250.00 in current 2014 value. He knew that this evening was not going to be inexpensive, but it was necessary. He counted out the money and handed it to her. She placed it in her handbag and smiled.

"Very nice, Gordon, thank you. Now we can have some fun." They spent the rest of the night in bliss and sleep. It was sweet, but transient in the scheme of things. And that's how it went for that first day in Hong Kong.

Meeting Aaron the next morning, then after breakfast down the street, Gordon and he decided to take the ferry across the harbor to Kowloon and the New Territories on the Chinese mainland. This trip, and other sightseeing venues, had been described in the ship's Plan of the Day provided before they had arrived in port. Reaching the other side, they took a bus to a designated mountain road, to an area as close as the vehicle was going to get.

They walked the rest of the short distance to the communist Chinese border. They stood there looking amazingly not across a fence or barbed wire but past several triangular signs painted red with black lettering, in Chinese and in English.

The signs warned visitors that this was the border; that no one should go any farther. The scene was so pastoral, looking down from the top of this small mountain, at fields of rice paddies, just like in the travel books, thought Gordon.

This was the '70s and not only was the cold war still on, but the People's Republic of China under Mao Tse Tung was a potentially fearsome adversary while the United States was still fighting in Vietnam. Gordon and Aaron were fascinated to be standing right there, to be that close to this international border in this historical context of war and uncertainty.

They traveled back across the harbor into Hong Kong, then stopped for lunch at one of the famous floating restaurants located on ferry-like vessels. This meal was much more conventional and far less dramatic than their previous lunch the day before.

After eating, Aaron said, "You know, since we're here in this town, we need to get tattoos."

"Tattoos? I wasn't thinking much about that, I was thinking about going back to the club to see Kim."

"The club and that tomato can wait, my friend, we can do that later tonight. Right now, we need to get some ink on us while we're here in Hong Kong."

Gordon really hadn't thought about getting a tattoo. Yes, he was a sailor and lots of sailors had tattoos, but lots of sailors didn't. Besides, it was unauthorized for sailors to get tattoos, with exceptions and other policies detailed as per the Uniform Code of Military Justice (UCMJ).

It was akin to defacing or destroying government property, or otherwise, depicting subjects or other artwork visibly on the body that could be deemed offensive. In spite of the regulations, many sailors opted to get tattoos.

For Gordon, it would take courage and imagination to get his tattoo, although at any time that he had thought about it, he had considered either an anchor, which he felt was traditional, a true mark of the sailor, or Betty Boop, the cartoon figure, which he felt was just fun and romantic. A cousin of his had served in the Navy during World War II and had about a dozen tattoos consisting of anchors, chickens, and other cartoons – it was completely out of control on his body and Gordon did not ever envision himself in that configuration. This was still the time in social history when it was unusual for people to have tattoos – only sailors and criminals had tattoos, not moms and teenagers.

Gordon and Aaron hailed a cab and went back to the Wanchai district. Aaron, who had been to Hong Kong before, knew where they were going.

Their destination was to "Pinky's," on Lockhart Road above the Neptune Bar, established by the world-famous tattoo master, Pinky Yun, now since deceased. By most accounts, he was the master.

By 1972, he had apparently already relocated himself personally to California, but he had shops in Hong Kong and in Japan. If anyone was going to get a tattoo in the Far East, his was the definitive shop in which to get it done.

They negotiated the stairs to the tattoo parlor on the second floor above the street level bars. They walked in and Gordon was overwhelmingly struck by seeing every inch of every wall covered with sample tattoos from which to choose from.

Even all of those weren't enough for him, and he sat down to begin looking through book after book of thousands of additional artwork. He saw traditional ones, modern ones, and outrageous tattoos. It was a tough decision.

Then he saw one that really got his attention – a beautiful Betty Boop, in a short, but demure black outfit, wearing a sailor's Dixie hat, sitting on the flukes of an anchor held by a trailing chain. It was perfect, just what he wanted.

"Hey, Aaron," he called over to him, "Look at this – I've got to have this one."

Aaron, who had already decided on getting a butterfly tattoo, all the rage then, was choosing his own, to be inked in an inconspicuous place on his back near his shoulder.

Looking at the sample that Gordon had chosen, Aaron agreed. "That is a righteous piece of work. Yeah, man, that's the one to get."

Now where to place it, thought Gordon. There really was only one place for this, on his upper arm. In order to look good, it needed to be at least three inches long – a big piece of real estate, but it had to be done right. He would just have to face his Chief Petty Officer and Division Officer when he returned to the ship.

Gordon showed the choice to the artist. "How much will this cost?" he asked him. The artist said it would be $35.00, which would probably cost about $125.00 today. Gordon was ready.

The artist traced the lines of the tattoo about two inches down from his right shoulder and started the process.

Three hours later, there was Betty Boop, with her dress, her hat, and she was seductively wrapped around a steel gray anchor. She was beautiful. He had gritted his teeth, and his fists were clenched throughout the ordeal, but it was worth it. Aaron had gone through his torment, which lasted about a half hour, with his teeth locked onto the back of the chair that he was sitting on.

They left the shop and stepped into the Neptune Bar for a nightcap. They were tired from the day and numb from their tribulation.

They weren't really thinking about partnering up for the evening. Instead of making a play for anyone in this bar, and since they were planning on meeting with their respective dates the next evening, as they were nowhere to be found anyway, they left the club and checked into a hotel room nearby.

Although they had originally thought about sleep, they were also hungry. It was a modern hotel and they called room service for some sandwiches. After a few minutes, an extremely lovely woman brought them their meals. As they were paying the bill, she asked, "Would anyone like me to give a nice massage by walking on their back?"

Gordon and Aaron looked at each other. The sandwiches forgotten for the moment, Aaron said, "Sure, why not?"

"Okay by me," Gordon agreed.

They took off their shirts and first Aaron stretched out and laid on his stomach. She hadn't mentioned money yet, until, while balancing herself on Aaron, she said brightly, "For $10.00 you can have sex with me." Aaron did not need a second invitation.

When they were finished, she started on Gordon's back. She took a few steps when he said, "You know, I could go for that special too."

"Sure, you give me $10.00 and we can have sex," she said. Gordon didn't hesitate either. Friendly though anonymous, she left soon after and they proceeded to eat their sandwiches, barely keeping awake through it, then they slept, nursing their new, still numb artwork.

Marked for life now with their new tattoos, they had culminated their R & R visit to Hong Kong with culture, love, and ink. The following day, their last, was spent shopping for various toys and trinkets to send home as gifts, then another evening at the club with their girlfriends.

Kim admired Gordon's tattoo, and seemed very familiar with the character of Betty Boop. Joanne wouldn't see Aaron's until they went back to her room. Each of them obviously did not mention their previous evening's liaisons to their dates, nor did their girlfriends mention where, or rather, whom they were with the night before. All they had to do was pay them in order to spend the night in their rooms.

It was pleasant for Gordon being with Kim for that last night. Although they hadn't really connected with each other on more than a superficial level, it was sincere for the moment.

Not that one could really get to know someone very well in just a matter of days, or even hours, however, sometimes people clicked a little more than less, even if they remained strangers. In spite of the lack of emotional depth, visiting this port was a completely memorable success in Gordon's mind.

Early the next morning, he collected Aaron as they said warm goodbyes to their partners in the breaking light. The women placed the men in a cab and they were on their way to fleet landing. Reaching the water taxi, they were paddled back to the ship, for getting underway in the next two days, back to the gun line, each with their new tattoos of distinction.

Crossing Over

Steaming out from Dakar, Senegal on the west coast of Africa, which had been the ship's first port of call for this deployment around the continent into the Middle East, the officers and crew on this U.S. Navy destroyer escort were headed next to Mocamedes, Angola. On their transit to Angola, they would cross the Equator, and would cross at the Prime Meridian, at 0° latitude and 0° longitude.

Crossing the Equator at any longitude is a unique and particular distinction for sailors, based on a very trying and rewarding experience, depending on how the ship's company performs this ritualistic initiation. Following the complicated ceremony, Navy sailors are rewarded with an "official," commercially produced certificate from Davy Jones and Neptunus Rex as issued by their ship, along with a wallet-sized card proclaiming their induction.

By crossing the Equator, their status changes from being a scurvy Pollywog to becoming a Shellback. Crossing at the Prime Meridian, however, elevates them to the enhanced level of a Golden Shellback. From lowly non-rated enlisted sailors, to non-commissioned Petty Officers, to high-ranking commissioned officers, they all have participated in this highly regarded Navy tradition, wherever in whatever ocean it was when they crossed. Most ships generally conduct this ceremony with the same major features, limited only by the imaginations of the sailors putting on the festivities.

The overall process first involves Pollywogs being charged by the Shellbacks with a crime or crimes, for example being a Liberty Hound or a Lounge Lizard. Not really too serious an offense, but an infraction for which a Pollywog is issued a summons by the Shellback committee. One would hope, however, that for the treatment that was about to be bestowed on a sailor that he or she was not someone whom people didn't like – this could be bad.

The morning of the crossing Pollywogs were awakened at 0400, including those watch standers who were also part that group who needed to be relieved of their watch for coverage by others. No one who has not crossed misses this ceremony when there is the opportunity to go through it. On this voyage, there were about forty sailors who hadn't crossed before.

Jeff Santos was one of these sailors and was looking forward to making the fabled transition. All of the rest of the approximately two-hundred and fifty officers and crew had been across sometime in their naval career and would be conducting the ceremony. Jeff, an E-5 / 2nd Class Petty Officer Electrician, was recently on board from his previous ship that had operated for the past two years in the Gulf of Tonkin off the coast of Vietnam, providing shore gunfire support, plane guarding and anti-submarine reconnaissance. The war was over, since 1975.

He had been in the Navy for six years, now on his second enlistment. An easy-going, competent technician, he was single, of medium build, standing 5'-6" tall, with curly black hair and dark eyes.

His eyes were usually focused on whatever was the task at hand. He would look at others straight on, concentrating on what they were saying.

He was respected and well-liked, both on this ship and on his prior one. He had quickly adapted to his new assignment, as a "salt" from the Far East and the Western Pacific fleet, having served in a combat zone.

He was assigned to A-Gang, working in several departments and divisions, responsible with other multi-trade non-rated and rated personnel for maintenance and repair of various auxiliary systems throughout the ship, such as electrical switchboards, communication circuits, compressors, air conditioning equipment, and for welding and plumbing.

His new ship was going to operate in various capacities along the African coast, throughout the Arabian Peninsula, and in the Indian Ocean. It was unknown if they would encounter any political unrest or other challenges that would test the military readiness of this ship and its crew, but for now, the Pollywogs would be initiated into one of the mysteries of the sea.

On this morning, the group of sailors was permitted to dress only in their skivvies, that is, their underwear, worn backwards. They were directed to go to the mess deck for breakfast. They had been warned that the meal would be different than regular chow. They might not have thought that it would be so barbaric that they would be denied a cup of coffee that early in the morning, but it was so – no coffee. That is a desperate situation for a sailor.

They could only help themselves to a big heaping plateful of green eggs (green!) and could only wash them down with a nice cold cup of tomato juice with plenty of hot sauce in it. They weren't taking this meal very seriously and most of them were laughing, especially the mess cooks serving the fare.

The previously elected Royal Sheriff, and his trusty Royal Dog, made sure that all of the Pollywogs took a plateful of eggs and a nice cup of juice. There was no escape. After "breakfast," they were taken above onto the bow of the ship and were made to sit quietly in a group, cross-legged while they waited for the sun to rise and for King Neptune and his bride to arrive. These characters were to be played by other Shellback sailors, along with the Royal Dentist, the Royal Lawyer, etc., who had been elected to these roles in a prior secret ceremony.

Upon the arrival of the Royal Couple, resplendent in home-made costumes, the Pollywogs were then forced to crawl on their hands and knees all the way from the bow to the helicopter deck, that is, the entire approximately four hundred foot length of the ship, while all of the time being whacked, more or less playfully (most of them, anyway), with short pieces of old, wet cloth-covered fire hose. Even the E-9 Senior Chief, the highest-rated enlisted man on board, got his licks in to the poor unfortunates, and relished it. Who said these sailors weren't mature, iron men of the sea? Officers, Petty Officers and non-rated personnel alike, they all looked ridiculous.

Once they were now assembled on the helicopter deck, one level above the fantail at the stern, each of them were then called upon to appear before the Royal Court members who were seated at tables, in order to defend their accusations. Fortunately, Jeff hadn't gotten charged with anything more serious than being a Lounge Lizard.

For this minor offense he had to kiss the toe of the Royal Baby which was completely covered with thick bearing grease. Next he had to take a drink of some more of that really vile hot tomato juice from the Royal Dentist.

Then, on their hands and knees, using only their teeth, the Pollywogs had to fish an oyster out of a spare toilet bowl that had been temporarily mounted on the deck.

Some guys had to take a swim in the Royal Bath Tub which was a small boat filled with oily, slimy water in which were placed many pieces of floating, rotting jetsam. For Jeff, though, he was permitted to participate directly in the final activity, that most glorious of tasks, a crawl through the garbage chute. This was a large plastic tunnel about ten feet long and three feet in diameter in which all of the mess deck trash from the previous week had been dumped into, really a wonderfully full, completely smelly finish to the festivities.

Leaving the chute, one Shellback sailor was standing by to hose those sailors completing the course with a spray of clean sea water, and then they could hit the shower. Jeff went below gleefully. He had done it!

There was very little else in Jeff's thoughts that compared to this sub-cultural, though world-renowned initiation ceremony. His exuberance was overwhelming. It was truly unforgettable. Only a select few multitudes of thousands have ever crossed the Equator with this much fanfare and prestige. Well, obviously not everyone would think of it in these terms. Jeff would just guess that one had to be there to experience it.

He and the other Golden Shellbacks received their certificates and cards from the ship's office several days later while the ship continued steaming south to their next port.

Jeff had crossed over from the Western Pacific and the war to the east coast of the United States, then back across the Atlantic, and now over the Equator. He was pleased that he had found a place on this ship to continue his world-wide seafaring journey, and was now ranked amongst the few, the honored, a member of this exclusive Shellback community.

Jewel of the East

Although while in Kenya on the continent of Africa the sailors on this U.S. Navy destroyer escort didn't have enough time to visit Nairobi, the capital city, or to climb Mt. Kilimanjaro, the tallest mountain, nor to go into the nearby jungle on a safari, ship's company would find enough diversions in this sultry coastal town of Mombasa to satisfy at least their carnal, if not cultural desires.

This was Lee Paxton's first time in this part of the world, in 1974. He had transferred a year before to this ship that was home ported in Charleston, South Carolina, from a more substantially sized cruiser. The cruiser was about half again as long and as wide as this escort which was only about four-hundred feet long by fifty feet wide. The complement of officers and crew on the escort would number even less than that on the cruiser, so Lee knew that he would still be able to maintain the comradery that he was accustomed to, and which he liked.

As a Machinist Mate 1ˢᵗ Class / E-6 Petty Officer, he was responsible for supervising the operation and maintenance of pumps, fans, turbines, and for running the watch crew operating the main engines, and electrical generators while the ship was underway. He was looking forward to advancing to Chief Petty Officer when his administrative and personnel management responsibilities would increase to having more direct interaction with selected department and division Commissioned Officers.

Lee had been in the Navy for eight years and would be re-enlisting for the next four in his commitment to career military. He was satisfied in his work and in his mission.

He had been married for the past five years to his wife Marianne. She worked as a legal secretary in Charleston, where they lived on the economy near the Navy base. Although she understood Lee's deployment schedule, and in the early days of their relationship she had a reasonably positive attitude about it, these days she was growing tired of it. She was not supporting him emotionally, and he didn't know how their marriage would turn out following this next deployment away from home.

While in the United States, his ship's assignments usually placed him north and south along the eastern coast for a few weeks at a time before tying up to the pier again in Charleston. The ship would stay in port for a few weeks between runs, and then as per their annual deployment, would get underway to travel across the Atlantic for up to six months in the Mediterranean, or in the Middle East for various naval operations. This was military standard operating procedure for a Navy "lifer" like Lee.

As was usual that morning two months ago when Lee was getting ready to embark across the sea, he had said to Marianne, "Well, honey, here we go again. I'm out there making the dough for us to live high on the hog."

"Don't try to be funny with that honey stuff, and living good," she had said. "While you're out there meeting the dames I'm here trying to stretch your lousy $500 a month E-6 money on top of that skimpy housing allowance you get."

"While you're sightseeing, I'm at the Commissary after work trying to feed myself and meet these bills. Never mind that I'm only talking to a bunch of other sailors' wives while they chase their children around the yard. I need something else to keep me going."

Lee was not surprised that she had said something. He knew she was less in tune with his schedule than she had been, and had spoken out before. Lee had tried to set her straight.

"Look, I'm not meeting any women, I'm not sightseeing. I'm spending sixteen hours a day, morning, noon, and night running the engine room and dripping my guts out in sweat. It's not fun; it's work. I'm doing all of this while you go to your job in a nice air conditioned office, having regular hours and eating ice cream whenever you want. You're killing me with your belly-aching. I don't need this. I need you to keep me happy while I'm on the beach, answer my letters when I write and maintain yourself as a pretty Navy wife. I'm glad you're working, and you have an interesting job, and you're bringing in your own money. Doing that until I come back should help keep you sane, doesn't it?"

"Well, if you think so. Maybe it should, but I'm just tired of being by myself. Maybe if I had a little boy or girl to run after while you're gone, I would be better until you get back."

He had heard her. "You know, you're right," he had said. "If I wasn't so full of myself I could see that. How about when I get back we figure this out? I really don't want to lose you."

"I don't know. I'm on the edge here. We've been talking for the past year about you shipping out, and then me being on the nest. I'm tired of the talk and something has to change."

"Okay, okay. Let me get underway this time without all the drama, and I promise I'll come back a changed man. I'm serious about this."

She just looked at him. Her hesitation in answering did not match his hopefulness.

"Alright," she had finally said. "I'll play along. But just make sure when you get back that you have it figured out what you're going to do to make me stay with you."

"I will do that," he had said.

So now, these two months later after leaving Charleston and having traveled across the Atlantic, the ship's voyages had taken them to several ports on the west coast of Africa. These included Dakar in Senegal, Monrovia in Liberia, and Mocamedes in Angola. At this time in the mid-nineteen seventies, following the quagmire of Vietnam and the cessation of ground combat there, the United States was not actively engaged in war operations in Africa or the Middle East. Based on this political climate, Lee, along with ship's company, had the opportunity to visit these ports, rather uneventfully, although always alert to the immediately shifting political climate.

Before arriving in Angola, they had crossed the Equator and had conducted the fabulous and famous Shellback initiation ceremony for about half of ship's company. Lee had crossed the Equator before this voyage and did not have to participate on the receiving end, but was able to give out with the ubiquitous, comedic punishment accorded sailors crossing for the first time.

Following the initiation, when they had arrived in Angola, their fueling requirements demanded that they take on 150,000 gallons of fuel to fire the boilers which took almost ten hours to complete since the fuel was being taken from tanks on a hilltop near the pier, at a paltry approximately 100 gallons per minute.

During this refueling, on the day that Angola had achieved its independence as a former colony of Portugal, there had been a report that the Angolan Army was mobilizing to forcibly take over this U.S. warship.

The crew and officers were placed at General Quarters, or Battle Stations. The fueling continued, with constant communications between the ship and Washington, D.C. This was the critical level to which this danger had escalated.

The evolution was handled by the Boiler Tenders. Fortunately, as deemed by the "Oil King," the Petty Officer responsible for completing this evolution, enough fuel had been replenished in order to reach their next port, and the operation was secured. The ship got underway without this threat coming to fruition.

In spite of the uncertainties, the crew's short liberties in various ports had involved some drinking, eating, and walking around these cities while staying relatively close to the waterfront, on the periphery of these city's exotic cultures. Although while in Dakar, Lee and several of the other Machinist Mates had also visited an international art museum, doing something more than just quenching their thirst.

During each visit Lee would be thinking about Marianne – what she might be doing based on the time differences, and what she might be thinking about since he left. She had not answered the four letters that he had managed to send out through the ship's post office. The ship had two mail calls since leaving Charleston. Neither of these times had Lee received anything from Marianne.

Leaving Angola after refueling, they navigated around the Cape of Good Hope at the tip of South Africa and steamed north off the east coast of the continent to Mombasa in Kenya, a former British colony.

The ship anchored in the harbor of this city. Small boats would ferry crew members ashore, in staggered groups based on watch sections. Lee and three other Machinist Mates went over by this launch. They would have this evening for liberty, with their return required for morning quarters at 0700 hours.

Landing, and then leaving the end of the pier, they took a cab ride costing twenty shillings, about three U.S. dollars, to the restaurant at the Mombasa Beach Hotel.

This location had been recommended by the information provided in the ship's Plan of the Day which was published on board daily. Besides noting reveille, scheduled drills, meal menus, and other operational data, prior to arriving in liberty ports the ship's Executive Officer, the second in command, would include tourist information, and selected guidelines in the Plan. This material would help sailors orient themselves to the places that they visited, and it would note sections of any ports that were off-limits, or that would otherwise be dangerous.

They had not been warned against any corrupt areas here in Mombasa.

Entering the restaurant, the maître 'de seated the group. Lee ordered cream of chicken soup, Kingfish, or swordfish, which shared the plate with an immense piece of cauliflower.

The group shared a bottle of Petit Duc Rose wine during dinner, had coffee, and then gin and tonic cocktails as they sat on the veranda overlooking the sea. Rather smashing, really, thought Lee.

He was also thinking again about Marianne, working now and maybe getting ready for lunch while he was eating dinner here at 8:00 p.m. He also thought about sharing this meal with her. She liked fish. They had eaten out so many times when Lee was in Charleston.

He really hoped that she would join him again when he got back this time, but he couldn't tell if he could make the grade to have this happen. Maybe it was time for him to move on, he thought. Maybe she was right in wanting to move on herself. It's not really what he wanted. He was not comfortable being in this position of uncertainty. He always thought he knew what he wanted, especially after he met Marianne.

Following dinner, they went to a nearby club named the "Casablanca" since one of the other sailors had been there before, and recommended it for its full bar and exotic women. The drinks were served from the bar, but in an open courtyard with a dirt floor, enclosed by white-washed stucco walls, brilliantly lit from the full moon.

The group sat at tables in the sweltering, calm night air and ordered Tusker lager, a popular beer. Before long, other sailors from their ship arrived and filled the empty chairs. As several friendly hostesses sat down among the men, they all struck up easy conversations, since everyone spoke English.

"Hello," said one of the women to Lee as she sat down next to him. She was dark-skinned, magnificently beautiful, with large brown eyes, wearing gold hoop earrings, and showing a friendly smile.

"Hello, yourself," Lee said, all thoughts of Marianne disappearing. "What's your name?"

"My name is Amina," she said. "Who are you?"

"I'm Lee. Pleased to meet you."

"Yes, this can be very pleasant," she said. "If you like, you can please buy me a drink?"

"Got it," he said, and signaled the bartender.

Lee wasn't thinking now about Marianne. He wasn't thinking at all, he was just relaxing in Amina's company.

"Have you been traveling long?" she asked.

"Not too long. We've been sailing for a few months but it's what we do."

"Yes, I know. We have had other ships come here from the United States. Many sailors come to this club."

"It's a nice, bright night," Lee said.

"Oh," she said, "small talk."

"Well, why not? We just met. What do you want to talk about?" By this time, her drink came.

"First, how about a toast?" she said.

"Sure. Here's to your beautiful country."

"That's a very nice thing to say. Have you been here before?"

"No, but from the little I've seen, and from what I know, it seems nice."

"Well, we have many troubles here," she said. "We have our very poor people and we have people of different tribes and groups who don't get along very well with each other."

"Yes, but you also have a long history of a great mixed culture, from Arabs with Africans, and English, and then a great struggle for freedom. That should count for something."

"I would have to agree with you, and I thank you for saying that. It seems you know some things about us. In my country here I am a princess of my people. But even as a princess, as a sparkling jewel, I have to work in this club."

"I'm sorry about that. I guess lots of people have things that they wish they didn't have to do, but they have to do them anyway."

"What about you? Is there something that you have to do that you don't like?"

"Not really. I like what I'm doing in the Navy, I like traveling, and I like meeting new people."

"You like me? Do I make you feel like you would like to be with me?"

"I would like that very much. You are beautiful and friendly. When you say you are a princess I would agree."

"That is very pleasing to me. I could teach you Swahili. I will say ninakupenda. Do you know what that means?"

"No, what did you say?"

"This means I love you."

Lee stopped short. He looked at her, and although she was striking and provocative, he was thunderstruck by the thought of Marianne waiting at home.

This exquisite woman sitting next to him, enticing him into a brief, superficial evening, as glorious as that might be, could not serve his needs as much as restoring his relationship with the jewel he left at home. He knew what he had to do.

"Amina, you're a really special and beautiful woman and I thank you for your attention. What I need to do now is to say that I had a wonderful but short evening with you, and I have to turn myself loose from your regal charms. It's a personal matter I must attend to."

"Oh, like that. I am not fooled. You are a married man, aren't you?"

"Yes, I'm married, and because you made me feel like one of a kind, I've got to take that same feeling and turn it back to my wife."

"I understand. I am sad for me, but happy for you, and your wife, to be true like that. It is something that you have to do. I will find another crown prince to be with me tonight."

"That's funny, Amina, to say that. Believe me, I was just this close to having my crown fall off completely when I met you tonight, but I'm glad you helped save me."

Amina stood up. "Goodnight, Lee. I'm going to go over there with some of your other shipmates. It was nice meeting you."

"Me too. Thanks."

Lee sat there quietly. Following a few more drinks and socializing, several of the sailors retired with their dates to rooms not too far from the club. But it was not cheap. The going rate for an overnight was approximately $100.00 U.S. For Lee, as a married man he usually avoided spending any money other than for dinner and liquid refreshment. He stayed at the table and finished his lager. Jimmy Kenton, an Electrician who Lee worked with, was sitting with him.

"What do you say we head back?" he asked Jimmy.

"Yeah, good idea. I've about had it."

"Aren't you sticking around to see what you can pick up for the night?" Lee asked.

"No, not for me, man. A little too rich for my paycheck. What about you?"

"You know me, buddy, I'm an old married man. I need to go back to the ship to write a letter to my wife, Marianne, to let her know I'm coming back."

"Sure, I get you. Makes sense."

"Yes it does," Lee said.

She Had to Leave and They Couldn't Talk

Richard Davidson drove slowly up the block. He was looking for Beth's house. He remembered the number but not exactly where it was. Then he saw it – a large, Queen Anne style home with two cars in the driveway. He found a place to park across the street.

Beth was expecting him. They hadn't seen each other since their college days, three years before. They had been friends, and had several mutually beneficial casual sexual encounters, but it hadn't gotten very serious. Even though their parting had been on less than the best of circumstances, Richard had always held on to the thought that they might get back together after he returned from Vietnam, where he had been in the U.S. Army for the past twenty-four months.

He had been in-country before being rotated back to the States in 1969. He had not been in a field combat position, but his MOS, that is, his Military Occupation Specialty as an Army Corporal, had been in ordinance supply for field artillery. He had been stationed at the Long Binh Post, one of the largest support bases in Vietnam, about thirty miles north of Saigon, to provide these logistical services.

Before he was drafted, he had been attending a small private college in New York City, maintaining the 2-S deferment available to full-time students in those days.

Although this draft designation was favorable to those who were accepted into college and could afford to go to school, it was an elitist category for males of draft age straight out of high school.

Once he ran out of money and decided to formally withdraw from classes, however, he received his 1-A status shortly thereafter, making him very eligible for the draft, and that's just what happened to him. Drafted, inducted, basic training completed, and then shipped to Vietnam.

His work at the Long Binh Post was not overly taxing and was rift with boredom and some discomforts, but it was tempered with an overwhelming amount of State-side type civilianized commercial and social amenities. The safety of this rear echelon position in comparison to the danger faced by the combat grunts searching and destroying the Viet Cong in the terrifying jungle was just that, relatively safe, although it was another very real part of the war. Sometimes the base would come under attack and sections of it had been destroyed by enemy fire just before he had arrived, but again, he wasn't in the boonies chasing the VC.

In those days before he was drafted, his time in college with Beth O'Brien had not been completely focused on the war. Although the war seemed to be enveloping more and more of the general landscape, for Beth and Richard they were basically concentrating on their studies and not much on their relationship, which was mildly passionate and more intellectual. The war had just been part of their environment until Beth became increasingly political against the war.

Although Richard was not overly attentive to the war, Beth did yield to the compelling need to put into action the growing awareness amongst college students and others in the national and global population that this war needed to be stopped and people needed to be stopped from participating in it.

In between Psychology, Art History, and sociable sex, Richard did express to Beth his growing discontent with remaining in school, especially since neither he, nor his family had adequate financial means to keep him there. They were walking to a class one morning to take a final exam when Richard brought up the subject of money.

"Beth, I'm really not going to be able to register for the spring semester," he said.

"Oh, what's the matter?" she asked.

"I don't have the money."

"What about your financial aid package?"

"Well, actually, with my dad's new job, my family's income, though not great, is just over the edge of placing us out of eligibility for enough to cover registration and my books. I've got to stop. Besides that, I'm not really focused on what I want to do, since I don't know what I want to do."

"You know what will happen to your draft status once you drop out, right?" she said.

"Oh, yeah, I know what's coming, next stop Vietnam, but I can't help it. Anyway, why should I be spared just because I can go to college? What about all of the rest of those guys out there who can't go to school and are in the same boat, facing Vietnam?"

"Richard, let's not talk about them, let's talk about you. You're bright and you can succeed in school, why would you give that up? Why would you put yourself in that spot just because of money?"

"Well, because money is a big part of it and I'm not feeling it here. I'm not accomplishing anything worthwhile enough to keep me here."

"So you think it would be more meaningful to just go to Vietnam?"

"I don't know if it would be more meaningful. It's just what's probably going to happen. I'm not the only one in this predicament. There are plenty of other guys out there who don't have a choice either."

She stopped walking and looked at him hard with her dark blue eyes. It seemed like her long red hair, falling straight to her slim shoulders, bristled with aggravation. Her slight frame seemed to rise, and she was facing Richard directly. Richard, also a slim man, stopped and backed away from her intrusion. He didn't do well in confrontations.

"You know, Richard, you do have a choice. You know that I'm doing draft counseling and I can help you avoid it, if you have the courage to take my advice. You know what I'm talking about, going to Canada."

Richard could not conceive of this action. He wasn't a committed patriot, but he had no stomach for personal insurrection against the government.

"I've thought about it plenty," he said, "but that's not really something I can do. My family doesn't do things like that. My dad served in World War II, so did my uncles and I just can't go that way."

"Maybe I won't go directly into combat anyway, not everyone does that you know."

"Well, I don't know about getting out of direct combat," she said, "I just know about what I see on TV and from what I read in the papers. You would be part of it. There's too many guys going over there and getting killed or mutilated, and for what? I can't see that for you. What does your family think about this?"

"They don't know what to do. They can see how bad this could be, but they don't know how it can be fixed. They don't know what to think about the war. They just know that a lot of guys are going over there and they don't know what to do about it, like a lot of people in this country. Beth, I see how you're looking out for me here but I just have to go with this. I'm not happy in school, unless I'm spending time with you. I just have to take my chances."

"Richard, I'm losing it here with you. Never mind being with me; there's no way I can support you in this. I can't see you going into the military in any shape or form. You are not Army fodder type. You need to stay in school."

"You know, you can say that all you want, but you're not facing what I'm facing. I'm in the same situation as all those other guys out there who can't afford to avoid this thing. Not everyone can. I had my shot after high school. Now I have to face it. I didn't expect that you would be happy with what I'm doing, but I thought you'd understand."

She looked at him for a long moment. "Well Richard, you do what you think you need to do but don't expect me to be in your corner. I'm against the war and against the military and against the draft."

"Sounds like you're against me, too."

"I'm not against you – that's just the trouble. I'm so much for you."

"Yeah, so much for me that if I go along with what you want for me, no, actually if I go along with what you want for you, to not have anyone go into the military, then you'll be satisfied."

"That is just what I'm talking about," she stabbed at him. "That is exactly it. No one should be going to fight in Vietnam, no matter what."

"Beth, you can intellectualize that view all you want, but the reality is that some guys just have to go, it's just that simple. It's too easy to just say don't go; don't let them get you, but it takes more guts than I have to figure out how not to do this than to do it. I even looked into the National Guard, but it's tough to get a billet these days and I'm not committed to going for a teaching degree even though teachers are exempt."

"I don't know, Richard, this is hard for me. I'm your friend and of course I don't want you to get hurt. I just can't get myself wrapped around what you're getting yourself in for. I hate the war."

"But you're not going to hate me, are you?"

"No, I can't hate you. I'm just feeling pretty sorry for you, and a little for us, too. I guess we'll be having a short happy life here at school," she lamented.

"It can still be happy," Richard said. "I'm not leaving to go anywhere yet. I'm finishing this semester and it could take awhile before anything happens. I'm going to look for work somewhere."

"No, Richard," she said, "now that you're making plans to be gone, I'm going to start fading, too."

"Wow, just like that," he said. "I don't know, how about supporting me until we see how this pans out?"

"Well, okay, to be fair and since we've been friends and involved, I'll stick it out for awhile, but I can see that we may disappear from each other soon," she said.

"I don't know," he said, "maybe we can keep this going, no matter what."

"Keep it going?" she snapped. "We'll see where that goes."

They continued walking in silence, until they reached their classroom, and did not speak again that day. This emotional scene had preceded their completing the semester. It led to stopping their infrequent liaisons, as Beth just couldn't reconcile Richard's acquiescence towards the military with her passion for dissent. And she couldn't be faulted for her opposition to the war – it was becoming abundantly clear that there was something wrong with American foreign policy that kept fostering this obsession with feeding the war in Vietnam.

The surrounding conflict and Richard's yielding to it finally led to their times together being completely broken off.

She was unwavering in her position as anti-war and anti-draft. Sadly, though, the negativity on her part, and from so many in the population then led to becoming anti-soldier.

This was the worst reaction, to not support the poor souls who really had such limited choices. They were the victims; they were not the enemy.

As the next few months went by after Richard closed the door on school, he was able to find a job moving stock and shipping records for a small music distribution company. The supervisor who hired him didn't focus much on his draft status, since the company just needed someone immediately who was willing to work hard.

It was shortly thereafter that he received his 1-A classification and went through the process of being medically examined for and then entering the military.

Just before he left for basic training, in amongst saying goodbye to various friends and relatives, he called Beth and she agreed to see him. It was a calm session, with some talk of him writing to her, to see each other again when they could, and they called it a night.

Richard spent the next year training in the States, then he served in-country at Long Binh. Responsible for ordinance supply and distribution to the various ground units operating in the area, he was not directly involved in combat operations, but was on the periphery as a link in the chain. Following a relatively uneventful tour of duty, he was rotated back to the States and separated from active duty. He returned to his family in New York.

The war was winding down, somewhat, with troop withdrawals commencing, however, the drafting of eligible personnel was still in effect. The South Vietnamese Army had the expanding responsibility of fighting against the North Vietnamese, with the United States participating.

The Navy's role continued in the Gulf of Tonkin, with shore bombardment by various surface ships and air strikes launched from several carriers in support of those troops.

For Richard, however, while the fighting may have been deescalating, the war wasn't over, and certainly wasn't over for military personnel when they came home. He didn't directly encounter the people who were spitting at Army, Marine, Navy, and Air Force personnel in uniform returning from Vietnam in the airports. He didn't encounter the people who were screaming, "Baby Killers!" at these returning veterans, whether they had been in the bush, or not, without these people having any idea of the veteran's service experience. Richard's turn for disrespect came in a milder form a little while after he returned to the States, or the "world" as those serving in the Vietnam theatre said.

When he had been home for a few weeks, and his family had made him feel welcome, he decided that he would see if anyone from former college days was available to visit.

He had corresponded only once or twice with two or three of his friends during the time that he was overseas. One of those friends was Beth, but it hadn't continued. They had left it in his last letter that he would call her when he came home. Richard thought that this understanding was still in place, so he called and that's how he was here at her house this evening. He walked up the front steps to the door and rang the bell. Beth's father opened the door. Richard had met him several times while at school with Beth. Her mother was not in the picture.

"Richard, how have you been? I heard you were back. Beth told me that you were coming over, and here you are. Good to see you."

"It's great to be back, sir. I've been gone for two years after I dropped out of school."

"How's your family doing?" he asked. "They must be glad to have you back. Are you alright? We've heard and seen so much about how bad it is over there. Are you okay?"

"They're fine and I'm fine. I didn't see much action, except for when they were firing at the base, but I never had to go into the field to chase the enemy. I had it way, way better then most, believe me. It was scary when they were shooting at us, but not horrifying. They never did get onto the base where I was. I'm alright."

"That's good, Richard. Again, glad you're back. Come on in and sit down. Let me call Beth. I'll tell her you're here."

"Thanks," Richard said.

He sat down on the couch. After a few minutes, Beth came down the hall stairs. He stood up to face her.

"Hello, Richard, how are you?" she said evenly.

"I'm okay, Beth, how are you doing?"

"Fine," she said curtly.

He was not surprised at her tone. Their telephone conversation the day before when they set up this date, no, this meeting, had been only polite, not exactly friendly. He would keep trying though – he had no agenda except to stand on his previous three year experience of enforced discipline and uncertainty and his memory of a time before that when they knew and liked each other.

"I know a club in the city where we could have a drink, if that's OK with you," she stated matter-of-factly.

"Sure, we can do that," he answered.

"Okay, let's take my car," she said. "I know where the place is down on the lower east side."

They drove across the Manhattan Bridge into the city. They spoke a little about what she had been doing after school, as an administrative assistant for a magazine publisher, waiting for a bigger break. She told him that during the past three years after he had left school and then shipped out to Vietnam, before she had graduated she had counseled and helped two former students to leave the country for Canada. He didn't react but told her a little about going over to Vietnam, but not much. This was his reality, not hers.

She wasn't that interested. He could see that this was a completely obligatory evening on her part and he didn't really know what he was doing here – just hanging on to an illusion of a blameless memory.

They parked on the street near the club. On the second floor, they walked into loud music, and sat at the bar. Richard bought the drinks.

They didn't say much. Sitting there in that noise, a man walked up to Beth, someone that she knew. She turned to him and introduced him to Richard.

"Evan, this is Richard who I used to go to school with. He's just back from Vietnam. Richard, meet Evan, a co-worker of mine."

Evan just nodded to Richard, then started talking with Beth, with her back to Richard.

Not a part of the conversation, after a while, Richard announced, "I'll be right back." Beth and Evan didn't stop talking to each other. Richard walked to the restroom through a door at the end of the bar.

When he returned, the drinks were there but Beth and her friend were gone. Just like that, he was by himself. So, that's how some of them treat the veterans, he thought.

"Do I owe you anything?" he asked the bartender.

"No pal, you're good."

Richard walked out the door, down the stairs to the street and looked around. The place where Beth had parked her car was already filled with another one. He knew where he was and considered taking the subway back to Beth's neighborhood to pick up his car, then decided to treat himself to a cab ride. He had a good amount of money from his Army separation pay and from what he had managed to save from an allotment. As an Honorably Discharged soldier he was entitled to apply for unemployment insurance, which he might do, or not. He would be alright for a few months. He walked to the busy corner of the block and after a moment, hailed a cab.

Should have known, he thought. What was he trying to hold on to? They had been gone from each other for a long time, different worlds ago. What the war had done to them. He was disappointed but not discouraged. He would continue to move forward.

When the cab dropped him off in front of Beth's house her father was on the sidewalk walking their dog.

"Where's my daughter?" he asked.

"We were at a club and she met someone she knew, then she took off. I'm guessing that she knew what she was doing."

"She just never got over that I went to Vietnam, but it really wasn't my fault."

"I guess you're right. I know it wasn't your fault. Too bad son. I know that you were friends in the old days, but I guess that's what they were, the old days."

"That's alright, it was bound to happen. It was tough enough to hold on to something as flimsy as this long-distance friendship, well this acquaintance anyway, so we just have to move on."

"Well, I'm sorry anyway," he said.

"Thanks. I appreciate that. Let me ask you this, do you remember Tony, a mutual friend of ours from those school days?"

"Why yes I do. He and Beth were still talking on the phone up until just recently. As a matter of fact his family opened a bar and restaurant not too far from here. It's on 20th Avenue near 65th Street. The name is, "Counterpoint.""

"Sounds good," Richard said. "It's still early, maybe I'll head over there."

"Sure, why don't you do that?"

"I will. Thanks again for your help and it was nice to see you again."

"Yes, it was good to see you, Richard. Please take care of yourself."

Richard started his car and then drove through the streets to the restaurant. Finding it and parking nearby, he walked in and looked around. From behind the bar, there was Tony himself coming towards him.

"Hey, man, how you doing?" he said excitedly to Richard. "I can't believe I'm seeing you standing here in my joint."

"Yeah, man, I can't believe it either. I'm glad to be here."

"How did you find us?" Tony asked.

"Well, I thought I would hook up with Beth since I got back from the 'Nam, but that wasn't meant to be. I saw her father a little while ago and he told me where you were."

"That is amazing. It's too bad about Beth. I know that you two had something going on in the old days."

"Well, we had something, but not enough of it," Richard said. "It was over back then and it's over even more now. I'll have to get over it too. How did you wind up owning this bar?"

"Well, after I graduated, it was tough finding a job. With the war still going on, there was that left-over noise about draft lottery numbers, but mine was pretty high so I didn't think they would get me. Anyway, just about when I was fed up with the job scene, my folks decided that they would invest some money in this place, so I went to work for them. Nothing came of the draft. This bar is a pretty good gig, so far."

"That sounds great. How about some of the crowd? How's everyone doing?"

"You know, since even before you went away there was a bunch of them who had no use for the war and for what you were going to do in it. They weren't then, and they're not now, any too fond of what happened," Tony said.

"What happened?" said Richard, raising his voice, "What happened?" he repeated. "What about what happened to me? Doesn't anybody have a clue about that? You think I wanted to go over there?"

"You think I wanted this? And I didn't kill no babies. I didn't kill anyone. I handled the ammo that probably killed people, but it wasn't directly me who killed them. I was just stuck in it."

"Yeah, I understand, but stuck or not, and I know it's not fair, but you sure were involved. That's enough for them. It's been a couple of years, and even though the war is still going on, maybe they've cleaned up their act. Believe it or not, it just so happens that Bennie, Sharon, Calvin and some others are back here in the dining room right now. They came in a little while ago. What a coincidence. Let's go in and see them," Tony said.

"Alright," Richard said, "I'm game."

Tony led Richard past the bar and through a doorway which opened into a small dining space. Six people were sitting at two tables and looked up when they came in.

"Hey everyone, look who's back in town, it's Richard, back from Vietnam," Tony sang out.

Silence. Not one of them said a word. They just stared at him. These were some of the same people whom Richard had gone to school with, or whom he had known through mutual friends just a short time ago - now a very long time ago.

"Hey," Richard called out, "Don't you see me? I'm the same guy who left school and got caught up in the craziness of the draft, but I can defend myself – I didn't kill anybody."

It just didn't matter. To them, Richard was like a diseased thing, something to be despised. It was happening to a lot of Vietnam veterans, and this hatred of them would continue for years. What a waste, and a very great sadness.

They didn't spit on Richard or throw garbage at him, but tonight's rejection by Beth and the ignoring of him by a stranger and then by these former friends was something that Richard could see he might have to live with.

"Come on, buddy, let me take you out of here," Tony said, and placed his hand on his shoulder. He gently led him out of the room. "Do you want a drink at the bar? It's on me, I own the place."

"No thanks, man, I've had enough for tonight. I'm going home."

"Alright, Richard, you keep in touch. Let me know if I can do anything for you. Don't be a stranger now that you're back." But Richard knew that he would likely always remain a stranger.

"That's okay, thanks. It's good to know that someone is still here for me."

"I got you man, you're not alone."

"Yeah, sure, I know. I'll see you around."

Richard turned away and walked silently out of the bar.

Amusement Parks

It was hot waiting at the flume boat ride. Roy Kingsley was standing on line with his sisters next to him, moving forward on this day at the amusement park. From earlier in the morning until now, the park had provided lots of rides for the three of them to enjoy. It was their day. No promise of anything other than their having a private time together had been revealed, until it would race into their circle at this ride.

As they moved farther along, Roy could sense someone moving along with them toward the two-seater boats. When they reached the attendant who was standing there to help them in, Roy directed his sisters into one boat. Then he climbed into the one behind them. The attendant helped another body to slip in next to him.

He looked sideways to see who it was and saw a Hispanic woman with jet black hair, parted in the middle, running straight to her shoulders. With dark eyes, copper skin, a slim body dressed in a tight blue tank top, with worn-out blue jeans, sneakers, and wearing small gold hoop earrings, she looked about twenty years old, and sexy. Roy thought that the flume ride was probably going to get that tank top and her jeans wet and clingy.

He called to his sisters, "Hang on kids, this is really going to fling us!" They turned around. All they said in unison was, "Yay!"

"I want this ride to last a long time," the woman said to Roy.

"Sure, we can go on this one again," Roy reacted, making something up. He didn't know what she was doing in this boat with him.

"Oooh, I would like that," the woman said.

"I'm sorry," Roy asked innocently, "I didn't catch your name."

"I'm Olivia, who are you?"

"Roy."

"Okay, Roy, and how is it that you're in this boat?" she asked.

"Well, never mind me, I'm here with my sisters. What's up with you? Why are you here?"

"Why are you out with your sisters?" Olivia asked again.

"I'm home on furlough from the Army for two weeks, before I head off to my next duty station, so we made up that I would take them out for some fun. I haven't seen them for about six months. I wanted to spend some time together. What brings you here?" Roy asked her again.

"That's nice, you're out with your sisters. I was here with a girlfriend of mine from school but when she called home before to see how her grandmother was doing, she wanted her to come home, so I just stayed. I don't mind being on my own. I thought maybe I could meet someone."

Roy thought this was pretty forward of her to say that, but he wasn't about to question it, since he could now be the someone that she met

Before he could say anything else, his sisters, Barbara, aged fifteen and Tina, aged twelve, looked back at him, both smiling.

The boats were moving towards a tunnel before they would shoot out into a spectacular plunge down the flume. They had been looking forward to being with Roy at this amusement park in New Jersey. As their older brother, now all of twenty-two, they were excited that he wanted to show them a good time. To them, Roy was all grown up, having been away from home and in the Army for the past two years.

Roy was a trim fit wearing his civilian clothes of a short sleeved green sport shirt, khaki slacks and casual shoes. He had blonde hair, cut short in military regulation, was clean-shaven, with light blue eyes, and of medium height. He looked all of his twenty-two years, not a day older. It was 1971. Roy had served one twelve-month tour as an E4 enlisted Corporal infantryman in Vietnam – he had seen some action and was done. He wasn't going back. The remaining one year of his enlistment would be spent somewhere in the quiet of the mid-west, and then he would be discharged.

It didn't seem that his sisters had focused yet on Roy's new seat partner. They were just looking at him and were still happy. Roy smiled back, but was split in his attention. He was already formulating the quick future that he hoped he could promote to win with the warm stranger next to him. He also thought about his primary mission here, to entertain his sisters, but his thoughts of this obligation were interrupted by Olivia who said, "Looks like we're going over the top!" as the boat broke free of the tunnel, stuck its nose way out, then dropped seemingly straight forward and down the water slide.

The short, swift plunge ended with a huge sliding splash at the bottom of the flume. Water shot up and over the boat. Most of the passengers were wet and screaming with delight and relief. The boat glided to a slow stop. As everyone started to climb out onto the platform, Tina said, "That was so great, what a ride!"

Barbara said, "Wow that was really fun!"

Olivia said, "I was so hot when I got on that ride. Now I'm cooled off real good."

Roy said, "Yea, that was something alright. Makes you want to go again."

"Oh, I don't know," Olivia said, "Maybe we should dry off and find something else."

Tina and Barbara looked at each other. They just seemed to notice that Olivia was talking and didn't seem to understand what this was all about. How could they understand? This wasn't in the plan for this day.

Roy noticed their hesitancy and said, "You know what? Why don't we all go on the bumper cars? It's just over there by the miniature golf." He hadn't yet introduced his sisters to his new companion, but things were happening too fast.

"Yay!" the girls said together again. The suggestion of another ride made them ignore Olivia's presence.

Olivia said, "That's fine with me, whatever you want, I'm with you."

Roy's thoughts were racing in two directions. It was always a dangerous thing for a man's conscience to deliberate on physical pleasure versus family or social responsibility – for some men this is very difficult. For Roy, it was disturbing, but not debilitating.

He knew that he needed to pay attention to his sisters' needs, but he had to pay attention to opportunity. Hopefully, he would find a balance.

The group walked to the bumper cars. Roy paid for all of their tickets. He helped Tina and Barbara into their cars, and then he and Olivia climbed into theirs. The two sisters seemed a little perplexed, but they were excited about the ride and just squirmed in anticipation in their cars.

Fast and furious, the music loud, and with a pounding, driving beat, they started racing around the metal floor. They bumped each other's cars, laughing, screaming. When the time was up, they climbed out and collected themselves at the exit.

Roy finally introduced the girls. "Olivia, these are my sisters, Tina and Barbara. Girls, this is Olivia."

The sisters first looked at each other, and then each one said hesitantly, "Hi."

Olivia said, "How you two doing? I'm having a good time with your brother, so let's have a good time together, okay?"

"Alright," Barbara said, "I guess so."

"Me, too," said Tina.

"Good, that sounds fine," Olivia acknowledged them.

"Yeah, sure, let's have a good time like we said," added Roy.

"How about some food?" Olivia asked.

"Sounds great, girls? Let's head over to that food stand," Roy pointed.

Roy took the girls' hands, and Olivia followed. "What do you want, girls?" Roy asked.

"I want a cheeseburger with French fries," Barbara said.

"I want a hot dog with French fries," Tina said.

"And how about drinks?" Roy asked them.

"Coke," said Barbara and Tina.

"Olivia, what do you want?" Roy asked.

"Let me take a cheeseburger with fries and a Coke."

"Okay, and for me, I'll go for a cheeseburger, fries and a Coke, too."

Roy waited briefly on line, then stepped up to the counter and placed the order. Olivia and his sisters just stood there, waiting, looking out at the rides across the park, and not talking. When the food was served, he called to them to start carrying the items, leading them to an empty table.

Once they were seated, they basically concentrated on eating. The girls seemed to enjoy what they were eating, but Roy could obviously sense by their strange quiet that they were not comfortable. Olivia didn't say anything either.

Once they finished and had cleared the table, Roy picked up the pace again and said, "Hey, let's head over to the Fun House. We can just walk through it and still keep our stomachs in place."

"Is it a scary Fun House?" Tina asked.

"I hope so," Barbara said.

"Is it okay if it's scary?" Roy asked.

"I would love it," Tina said.

"Me, too," Barbara said.

Olivia said, "I could do scary. I'm not afraid of anything." Roy was not surprised.

They entered the Fun House, basically made up of a section of rocking floor, moving steps and a dark maze. The girls did seem to enjoy themselves, and Roy and Olivia were able to stay close to each other. As the afternoon went on, Roy tried hard to concentrate on his sisters, but Olivia was definitely a distraction. Finally, after two more hours of roaming the park, playing some games of chance and going on some more rides, it just felt like it was time to wind it down.

"Girls," Roy said, "Have you all done what you wanted to?"

"I'm good," said Tina.

"I've had about enough," Barbara agreed.

"I'm ready to leave," Olivia said.

"OK, then we go," Roy said.

Roy had not yet asked Olivia where she was leaving to go to. He was just captured in the madness of this glue. They walked to the parking lot, to Roy's father's car, a 1965 Chevrolet Impala which he had borrowed for the day. Roy opened the car and his sisters climbed in the back while Olivia stood next to the car.

Roy said, "Olivia, we're headed to Brooklyn. After we do that, I can take you somewhere. Where would that be?"

Olivia said, "I live in East Tremont, in the Bronx."

"I can make that," Roy said. He was completely stuck in lust gear and would have taken her anywhere. From Brooklyn to the Bronx was that kind of distance – about twenty miles to anywhere. Barbara and Tina didn't say anything.

Olivia sat in the front seat and Roy started the engine. It was hot in the car without air conditioning and they all opened their windows. They headed slightly north to the George Washington Bridge to cross the Hudson River, then south through Manhattan to the Brooklyn Bridge, to cross the East River.

On the way home, they had listened on the radio to Joan Baez's cover of Mickey Newbury's song, "It's the 33rd of August," which included, for example, the lyrics, *'Once I stumbled through darkness, tumbled to my knees, but now I've got my dangerous feelings under lock and key; guess I killed my violent nature with a smile.'*

It was not so much that the song was haunting and mysterious, which it was, but that the karma tied to listening to this song on the date of this excursion in the park was September 2nd – the 33rd of August.

They traveled on the Belt Parkway that circled the Borough of Brooklyn, then exited the highway to reach the neighborhood where Roy's family lived.

He parked the car on the street and they walked to the apartment building, Roy thinking to drop off Barbara and Tina.

Roy wasn't sure yet what he was going to say to his mother and father about Olivia if they were home, but he was counting on their reluctance to challenge him, since he was recently back from the war and would be home for only a short time.

He did expect to deliver his sisters, and, although the girls were quiet on the way home, he was hoping that they were still in good spirits about being out for the day.

As Roy turned the key in the apartment door, he didn't hear his mother or father inside. Barbara and Tina were standing behind him, with Olivia standing along a wall in the hallway.

"Anyone here?" Roy called. No answer. Barbara and Tina ran past Roy into the apartment. Roy reached behind him and guided Olivia through the doorway. She moved inside the hallway. His sisters had disappeared farther into the apartment. Roy led Olivia to the left into his bedroom and closed the door.

Although he figured this would be a relatively quick visit in the apartment, he could always hope that she would just melt into his arms once they were alone – well almost alone. He really wasn't thinking very logically, but there had been nothing about this day with this woman that had been very logical to Roy.

"So, this is where you live?" she said somewhat vacantly, her voice trailing off.

"Well, I haven't been here much for the past two years. I've been over to Vietnam and places in between," he said.

"I don't know much about Vietnam, just what I've seen on TV," she said. I don't have any brothers, just two sisters like you, so my family hasn't been bothered much. Some of my friends' families have guys who've been there, but they're back, too."

There wasn't much here that Roy could tell were any thoughts in his favor from Olivia. Whatever she was looking for on this day he just couldn't figure out, but he didn't need to do that.

He just needed to find out if he could use her like she was using him – that's about as far as this was going for him.

She looked around the room as they stood there. "Why don't we sit down?" she said. This was too easy, he thought.

"Sure, come over here," he said, taking a step to the bed. They sat down on the edge of his bed. She reached over and pulled his head towards hers, and they kissed for a long time.

He sank back onto the bed, holding her, kissing her, and he initiated some preliminary groping. She responded in kind and they were at it for a few minutes when they heard Tina calling.

"Roy, do you know when mom and dad are coming home?" she asked.

Roy sat up to reality. "No, I don't remember what they were doing today when we went to the park, but they must be close since we have the car," he called through the door.

Olivia said, "Look, we can't get much done here, how about we head down to Coney Island and get something to eat? Then we can do something else."

"Okay, if that's what you want," Roy said. Could he have been more in? He would have to wait and see. There seemed to be some promise here but not at this moment. It could go the other way. Roy was captivated, but wasn't at all sure of the outcome.

He left Olivia there and walked out of his room, down the hall and into the kitchen. Barbara and Tina were sitting at the table, having glasses of milk with cookies.

"I'm leaving with Olivia," he said to them. I'll be back later and we can talk about our day at the park."

"Not much really to talk about, but if you want to," Barbara said to him glumly.

Roy just looked at them. He knew he should have shaken Olivia off a long time ago, but he was hypnotized by today's events. The cloud was shifting now, however, but he still wasn't done – this could still turn out to be good for him. But no matter how it turned out, it didn't seem to be going very well for his sisters. He told them where they were headed and left.

He and Olivia went out to the street. They drove to Coney Island, about a half-hour away, and found a place to park. The area was brightly lit, hot and crowded.

They skipped the rides, but headed into one of the arcades and played some skee-ball, pin-ball, and pitched some baseballs. Of all things, Roy won a small doll for her. Oh, he was so in. He could only hope and see if it was to be.

They took a break from the games and went into "Nathan's Famous" hot dog restaurant. She ordered two fried clam sandwiches, French fries and a beer. Roy ordered the same. They were sitting at a small round table squeezed in amongst the crowd.

They didn't talk much about anything; they just ate and drank. Roy still wasn't sure if he was going to score tonight or not. He felt like he had been attentive to Olivia and way more accommodating than anyone could have been, with rides, food, transportation, and a prize – but maybe he was going to be the prize fool.

About this time, Roy's money was beginning to run out. It was finally time, now about midnight, to drive her home to the Bronx.

Way up northward in the Bronx to the East Tremont section, somewhere, nowhere, to Third Avenue and East 180th Street, more than twenty-five miles from Coney Island.

They still didn't talk much on the way there. They listened to the radio and basically looked straight ahead. Roy was still hoping that he was taking her home to some private place where they could continue, and complete, what they had started way back in the early part of the day and then on his bed.

He stopped the car at the curb where she pointed. Olivia leaned over to Roy, gave him a quick kiss on the lips, opened her door, stepped out of the car and tossed the doll prize onto the passenger seat. "I'll be right back," she said.

Roy waited for awhile after she disappeared into the street scene and entered the door of an apartment house. He watched as one of the neighborhood youth crossed the street and turned in the alarm for a fire raging at another apartment building nearby. He watched as a drug deal went down at the corner. He watched as other people walked along the street. It was 1:30 a.m.

After watching and waiting for almost a half-hour, he guessed correctly that she wasn't coming back. Their romance was over.

His hoped-for tryst was not to be, after all of that effort, after all of that longing. *Fool that he was, he thought.*

He also thought about his sisters, but knew that they were too young to understand that one's flesh sometimes does not always have a conscience.

He thought about the waste of time and money that this day had cost him being involved with Olivia. He thought about the better time that he could have had with his sisters, if he hadn't been distracted by temptation. The doll was lying on the seat next to him. For as long as he would keep this doll, he would be reminded of this day. He tossed the doll out the window.

As he started the car and pulled away from the curb, turning around the next corner to head south, his resolve was firm. He knew that he was going to offer to take Barbara and Tina out again, just the three of them, if they wanted to, without interruption, before he would be heading back to the Army to finish his service time. He hadn't been able to cash in on this strange day with Olivia, but he hoped that he could redeem himself with his sisters. Their next time out would stay on course.

After Schoolwork

Dianne Mackenzie was a student during the day at a small two-year Community College in the center of a big city, and worked full-time from late afternoon to early evening dispatching trucks and clerking for a mechanical contractor. At twenty-four years old, she could be called pretty, but very plainly. A Scotch-Irish brunette with green eyes, she wore her hair loose to her shoulders and looked relaxed in her typical outfit during warm weather of clean worn-out blue jeans and a tee-shirt.

Her 5'-6" frame exploded with confidence in a steady, measured way of looking right at you, welcoming most anyone to share in her upbeat, though reserved attitude. She could always count on herself to face the daily challenges of her commitment to formal education, working hard at her job and living on her own. She was going to be a Psychologist, the first in her family to be on the professional path out of the scrabble of the working class.

She lived in a busy neighborhood a few blocks away from her mother, in the rental apartment that her grandmother had lived in before she died, when Dianne was nineteen.

Dianne had been mature and independent since she was fourteen, having sex, taking care of her mother, younger brother, sister and herself, after her father died.

She had always been employed at something, was well known in the neighborhood as a reliable family girl, had lots of friends and knew the score. She had determined where she wanted to go in life and had figured out how to get there.

Seth Martin attended the same college as Dianne during the day and worked part-time at a plumbing supply house on a varying schedule. At twenty-six years old, he was going after a way to stop turning pages in a parts book to begin turning pages in a bank book. Now in 1973, a year out of the Army after three years as an engine mechanic in the motor pool at an in-country base while the war in Vietnam dragged on, taking business courses would be the ticket to owning his own service shop.

Somewhat stocky but trim, he stood 5'-9" with short, well-combed blonde hair, and blue eyes in a face defined by thoughtful appraisal. Of German and English descent, he was focused, methodical, and poetic. His clothes didn't differ much from the type of outfit he wore to class, from what he wore at work – sturdy blue jeans, black work boots and a plain cotton shirt with the sleeves rolled up, a pack of Lucky Strike cigarettes and a pen carried in the top pocket.

Most of his transitions overlapped at these activities of school and work and he was usually short on time. He lived at home with his divorced father and two older sisters, enjoying being with his family after the Army, for a while.

He was supplementing his part-time work with a small stipend provided under the GI Bill while he went to school, and a small amount of money he had managed to keep from his separation pay.

Dianne and Seth didn't know each other at this college when they first started there, Dianne after working a few years out of high school and Seth after continuing his hand at a manual trade after the military. It was each of their third semesters there when they first met.

Waiting on the same line to register for a required Art History class one fall, on a bright, spacious day, he was standing behind her, hovering over a schedule, his eyes drifting to her neat figure. He moved closer and looked over her shoulder. People could do that on a class registration line.

"It's tough sometimes when the class you want gets closed out," he mentioned to her back factually, charmingly.

She turned slightly towards him. "Yes, it's happened to me plenty of times," she agreed, not unfriendly.

He sensed promise. "Do you know who might be teaching this class?" he asked.

She turned a bit more. "No, but with Art History there's probably only one or two professors anyway."

He moved just a little closer and said, "Well, I need this course to finish the last of my Liberal Arts requirements." He didn't say it negatively, just with resignation.

She didn't seem to mind his acquiescence and said, "It's just about one of my last ones, too, but I think it'll be pretty interesting. I don't mind."

He went on, "I guess, but I just want to get this one out of the way so I can get on with my business courses."

"Oh, that's what you're going for, Business Management?"

"Yep, I've got a plan – how about you? Business for you, too?"

"No, Psychology – my own practice one of these days. I need to go on to a four-year college after this degree."

"That's great. That takes commitment and focus, I admire that."

"And you, working in business, or owning your own business?"

"Ownership – I work for someone now and don't care much for it. How about you, are you working?"

"Yes, I'm a dispatcher for an air conditioning service company," she said.

"That's a coincidence, sort of, I'm working for a plumbing supply outfit – I guess we're related!"

She laughed. She seemed interested. He was smitten.

"You know," he said, "there's a chance we could be in the same art class."

"Maybe," she agreed, more positively than negatively, as far as he heard.

They moved closer to the registration desk. They seemed to be moving closer to a date. Getting to the card boxes, she registered with one of the student aides, he registered with another, and not in the same section, since one of the classes had just filled up. Even still, they were now almost colliding towards a date. They heard each other's names as they registered.

"That's too bad, we didn't get the same class," he said. "But now that we got through that, do you have time for a cup of coffee, or whatever it is that you drink?"

"Actually, I have one more class to go for, Social Psychology, then I'll be finished for today, until I have to get to work at one o'clock. If you want, why don't you stick around and we can have coffee after I hopefully get this class." She was even-toned, but he heard provocative.

"Okay, I'm game. I'll just follow you."

"Okay, let's go."

Registration for her class took another fifteen minutes. Standing together on line, they chatted idly about school, work, time management, food, a little bit of family.

She was a step ahead of him in planning, she was serious and friendly. He was straightforward about things, reservedly witty and strong, but he could drift. She seemed to know where this meeting was going for her.

He knew where he wanted this to go for him, but couldn't tell if it would. After she registered, they walked to the cafeteria in the same building, continued talking, bought coffee and sat down. He lit up a Lucky Strike cigarette; she took out a pack of Winston.

They sat there for another fifteen minutes, more talk of school, ambitions, her grandmother, his sisters, the war and his Army service.

Finishing up, she said, "Seth, I've got to get going."

"Yeah, I know, you said. I'm off today because of not knowing how long registration would be. Fortunately, I've got a pretty understanding boss and it worked out. Usually I'm tied up between school and work. Tell me, if you're not busy tonight, maybe we could grab a bite to eat." He stated this invitation without much request, more as a progressive fact.

"Well, I get off work at nine tonight. If you want, we could meet somewhere and then do something," she said. He thought he heard her unmistakable intent in this statement.

Noting that it wasn't going to be a meet-the-family night, he said, "Alright, how about I catch up with you at, well, do you know the Green Trim Cafe near here on Sanford Street at Bradley Avenue?"

"Sure, I've been there. Let's say about nine-thirty."

"Great, Dianne, sounds like a plan."

He didn't even consider that he needed her phone number, he knew that she would show. They walked out of the building to the parking lot, exchanging a few final words. They stopped, she went her way and he went his to their cars. It seemed to have been a productive morning for them both.

The rest of his day was a lazy haze of anticipation. The rest of her day was a busy time of responding to service calls, sending trucks on their way to repairs, and expectation.

He sat at a table in the Café reading the menu. It was 9:35 p.m. She walked in, they spotted each other; he stood up and smiled.

"Hi, Dianne, how did it go at work? Busy?"

"Hi, Seth. It was the usual. It's the season, lots of service calls. My company covers a lot of territory, but it's over now."

"That's good. Over, I mean."

"Yes, and I'm hungry. Have you picked anything yet?"

"Actually, I thought I'd go for something like a breakfast at this hour, bacon and eggs, coffee. I'll give you a chance to look over the menu."

"That's okay, I know what I want." And she did.

They ordered, she a hamburger with French fries and a milkshake. They talked about their neighborhoods, high school, handling family emergencies, cars, his Army service, the war, previous jobs, and various beliefs.

She ordered coffee and they smoked their cigarettes. This went on for about an hour. It was getting late.

"Seth, if you don't need to be somewhere, how about a second cup of coffee at my house?"

She was moving faster than him. He didn't mind; he was along for the ride. It hadn't dawned on him yet that he was being drawn into something serious – even she didn't realize it yet. She seemed pretty casual; he was more paced. This was still, however, moment by moment for both of them. It felt good to go with it.

Since they had come to the restaurant in separate cars, they left that way. Dianne told Seth where she lived; he knew where it was, but followed her anyway.

Her apartment wasn't too far from the school and remarkably, was only about a mile away from where he lived.

Finding a place to park, she waited for him in front of her building and he joined her after several minutes. They went inside. She lived on the second floor of a three-story building, above a row of stores. Walking in, he smelled bath powder and flowers. It would always smell that way, a loving, lingering reminder of Dianne's grandmother. She told him she liked it that way.

Surveying the small entrance foyer, leading through a hallway, past the tidy eat-in kitchen, to stand in the living room, he said, "Well, this is a nice layout. I can see why you took over the place after your grandmother died."

"It is nice, and it's convenient to shopping, my work, the rest of my family, and I've lived in this neighborhood all my life. Why don't you sit down and I'll put on some music."

He went over to the couch and sat on one end. She walked over to a cabinet next to a stereo set with large speakers and a turntable. She looked on a shelf and pulled out an album. He was watching her move around. He liked what he was watching. She knew perfectly well that he was looking at her. It was one of her expectations.

She turned the unit on, took the album out of its jacket, lifted the needle arm and placed the record on the platter.

He immediately recognized the Moody Blues album, from 1969, *On the Threshold of a Dream*. Tracks included *Lovely to See You, To Share Our Love,* and *Are You Sitting Comfortably*. Perfect.

"That's a great choice, Dianne," he said pleasantly.

"I like the Moody Blues a lot. I have all of their albums. How about you? Is this OK?" she asked.

"Me too; I have a bunch of their albums, and I really like them. They're soothing and philosophical at the same time. Great music, with that orchestra behind them"

"I know, there's something about them." I really like their '67 release, *'Days of Future Passed,'* with the cuts *'Dawn is a Feeling,'* and *'Tuesday Afternoon.'"*

"That's one of my favorites," he said.

"Yeah, and that's the album that has, *'Nights in White Satin,'* what a song."

"How about the one from about 1966 with their first big hit *'Go Now.'* That is an incredible record."

"Absolutely," she agreed.

She walked over to the couch and sat down near him while the album played on. They sat there quietly, listening to the music and to each other breathing. After the first side she got up and turned it over. He watched her do this and turned thoughts over in his mind. She sat down again, just a little closer.

"I haven't put up any coffee," she said at the end of the album.

"That's alright, I wasn't thinking about coffee," he remarked casually.

"Do you want to see the bedroom?" It wasn't a question; it was an invitation.

"Sure."

She turned off the stereo. They walked through the living room into the bedroom. She turned on a night table light. There was a double bed, a dresser, a chest of drawers, a TV and some family photos. The walls were painted a cream white like the rest of the apartment.

"This is pretty cozy," he observed.

"It's really comfortable," she responded. "I kept my grandmother's furniture, but got a new bed. Would you like to feel how soft it is?"

He stood perfectly still for the briefest of moments to focus on what he was hearing, and then he slowly sat down. She sat next to him.

"This is nice," he stated, without struggling to balance the waiting for her with the taking of her. There was no doubt where this would lead. They were adults; they were allowed to do this.

"Glad you like it," she said. "You wouldn't mind if I take off my sneakers after a long day, would you?"

"Here, let me help you," and reached down to her feet.

She unfolded herself, stretching out across the bed. He untied her sneakers and pulled them off. Sitting back up, he approached her face across her body and kissed her.

She kissed him back and, after some preliminary stroking and fondling, they progressed to gently removing each other's clothes, and to exploring each other.

It was a fine, satisfying evening for both of them. They slept, they were at each other again later, and they slept again.

Early the next morning, they had some fun showering together, then she put breakfast together. They did some more talking about work, school, family, the city, war, and then exchanged more romantic tenderness.

Around noon, Dianne announced that she needed to get to work. Seth didn't need to be at work until the next day and school wasn't scheduled to start for another week, so they decided to meet for dinner at the Café later that night.

Getting ready to leave, Dianne said, "Seth, this was great. You are a very nice man."

"I'm glad you feel that way. I like you. You're easy to be with and very competent. I like that in a woman. I don't know where this is going, but I like where we've been so far."

"I know what you mean. If that's how you feel, me too."

They left her apartment and kissed each other goodbye in front of the building. They walked separately to their cars. The day went by, dreamily for them both, full of feelings and possibilities.

It was 9:30 p.m. that evening. He was in the Café. She walked in and sat down.

"Hello, Seth, good to see you."

"Hey, Dianne, how are you?"

"Everything's fine, I'm just a little tired after another day in the salt mine," she said whimsically.

"I know, it can get to you. Not to me today, though, I didn't do much of anything but think about you."

"You're sweet. I'll be looking for some relaxation tonight after we eat." She wasn't shy.

"Works for me," he said brightly.

They ordered and ate, had quick cups of coffee with cigarettes and left the restaurant, again in two cars.

Once inside her apartment, Dianne placed an album on the stereo, *Led Zeppelin I*. This one was from 1969 with the cuts *Good Times, Bad Times,* and *I Can't Quit You Baby.*

"Great album, Dianne, another good choice. I am real partial to Led Zeppelin."

"Yes, there's nothing else like them." I've got a lot of their albums. You?" she asked.

"I have the one you have on, and I also have '*Album II,*' also from '69, you know, with '*Whole Lotta Love,*' and '*Heartbreaker.*' That is great stuff."

"I've also got *'Album IV'* from '71, with *'Stairway to Heaven,' 'Going to California,'* and *'Black Dog,'* he continued. "They are great."

"I have those," she said, "and *'Houses of the Holy,'* with *'Rain Song,'* and *'Dancing Days.'* They released that one just this year. I'm glad you like them. Makes it easy for what we're listening to."

"And you really know your albums," he said. "I'm impressed."

"That's okay, it's not much, but thanks."

Dianne went into the kitchen and came back with a bottle of red wine, a corkscrew, and two glasses.

"Let's open this," she said.

"Oh, that's nice. I can always have some wine," he agreed.

They sat on the couch, closer to each other than they had been the night before, listening, breathing easily.

Smoking cigarettes and drinking wine would just be incidental to them both. It was only a part of their activities, not major events.

They didn't finish the album side. She stood up, took his hand and wordlessly led him into the bedroom, leaving Led Zeppelin play on with the wine on the coffee table. They had another nice evening there in the coziness of that bedroom.

The next morning went well. They showered, had breakfast, and left the apartment together. He was off to work, while she was to run some errands before her afternoon shift.

They planned to meet that night. This time, though, they made up that Seth would just go directly to her house, skipping eating out. He would just get there after he figured she had arrived home.

Their meetings and dates were comfortable for the next week. Dianne cooked some meals. They went out to eat in her neighborhood, went to some movies, and played pool at the local bar, meeting some of her friends.

Once the school semester started, then they met as often as schoolwork and employment would let them. It wasn't a big stretch, though. Seth was only taking two classes; so was Dianne. They made time to be with each other.

They spent close evenings at her house listening to more of the Moody Blues, like the album *A Question of Balance*, from 1970 with the songs *How Is It We Are Here*, and *Dawning of the Day*. They listened to another album, *Every Good Boy Deserves Favour*, released in 1971 with the cuts *The Story in Your Eyes*, and *Nice to Be Here*.

The wistful, rhythmic mix of Moody Blues and Led Zeppelin in that comfortable apartment would be something that Seth would remember forever about those days. More than ten years later, he would hear the song, *Your Wildest Dreams*, on the Moody Blues album, *The Other Side of Life*, and would listen to the haunting lyrics, *"Once upon a time, when you were mine; I wonder where you are, I wonder if you think about me."* There would never be a time that he would not think about her when he heard this song.

A few weeks after they started going together, they briefly met each other's families and that was fine, though they didn't need to be involved with them too much at this point. Then, the next several months took on a routine of mutually agreed upon repeat activities.

They went to school, went to work, afterwards they went to the movies, or to one or two of the local bars. They continued talking to each other, they listened to music, and they had sex.

Dianne was satisfied to be with Seth as a companion and sexual partner together with her current activities as an independent woman pursuing her mission to become a professional. Dianne thought Seth was a good-looking, dependable man, but she had been on her own for a long time and wasn't bothered by not being married or cemented into a clinging relationship.

She didn't think a lot about a long-term relationship, there was time enough for that later in life. At least that's what she thought she believed in her mid-twenties. She was usually only thinking about having a good time, even though she was serious about moving forward.

Seth was more than content to be with Dianne for company, conversation, and sex. He interpreted his time with her as the way it was supposed to be while he was in his mid-twenties and for what he thought he was looking for, a match with a woman who was focused, bright and fun, for whom he was important to her, he thought, and for whom he could provide comfort and protection.

He thought about what it was like before Dianne, in his several connections with other women. These were just preludes to how he thought it should be, and was now with his relationship with Dianne.

One evening she received a phone call from an old boyfriend of hers. They had been involved for more than two years, a long time ago, before Seth. She hadn't mentioned anything to Seth about this former relationship.

The boyfriend had gone away to school, moved to another city for work, but was now back in the neighborhood. It didn't take a lot of soul-searching for Dianne to agree to go out with him one night. She was flexible and adventurous.

Her old boyfriend was currently employed as a copy editor for a small magazine publisher, with a great future. She could be loyal to Seth, for a time, but she could also be loyal again to her old love.

It didn't take long for Dianne to find a renewed link with him, after juggling two weeks worth of alternating days and nights with each of them. She couldn't help it and didn't need to. Part of her previous life was in front of her and she embraced it. She wasn't sure what it was all about yet, but it was exciting and comfortable. She hadn't invested a lot of time or heart-wrenching emotion with Seth; it was just an interval to her.

It was with some degree of effort, but not with a large struggle, that she was able to tell him that it was over. On a quiet evening following her being with her old boyfriend, Seth arrived at her doorstep.

She was going to be clinical with her emotions. He made it through the door. She stopped him at the kitchen. Standing there, facing each other, before Seth could speak anything else after saying hello, Dianne spoke.

"Seth, I don't really want to drag this out, but I've got to tell you that I've met up with an old, old boyfriend of mine, someone I went with for a long time, and, well, I'm letting him back into my life. I've reached the end of where we're going with us. Like I told you, you're a really nice guy, but now I'm just looking to move on. I don't know what else to say."

He stood there and thought he heard what she said. Then he did hear what she said. He was not overly emotional about things, he was usually disciplined, and in control. But the poet in him took over and this one got to him.

He looked straight at her. "Dianne, it sure seemed like we had something going here. It doesn't make much sense, but we're grown-ups. I will have to handle this. I guess you know what you're doing. I thought I knew what we were doing."

She stepped back a little. "I think I know what I'm doing, for me. Anyway, I hope so. I'm not going to forget these past few months with you, Seth. You were good to me and we had a blast but, well, I don't want to kill this; I just want to have it fade away peacefully."

"Okay, Dianne, I'll have to move on. You know, we won't be able to avoid it, but we'll probably see each other at school while we finish up this semester on our way to classes and work and all. How about we just nod to each other and say hello like fellow students and we'll pretend it's just fine? We'll just be like people we used to know. And I do mean pretend, because I can't help it, but I know I lost someone pretty special and I'm hoping that you know that for you, too. Dianne, please take care of yourself, and I'll see you."

They hesitantly moved closer and kissed gently. Seth turned, walked out of the kitchen, through the hall and out of the apartment. She closed the door softly behind him.

Pay the Price

"Hey, Jimmy, let's go!"

Mario tried it again. "Jimmy, come on!"

He was calling up to the second floor while standing on the sidewalk in front of Jimmy's building, a three-story row house along a grimy block in the Bedford-Stuyvesant section of Brooklyn. It was 7:00 a.m. on a hot summer morning, and it was time to go to work.

There were two other passengers in Mario Cantina's car, waiting for Jimmy Aspen to come down. Mario knew that Dean and Scotty wanted to get going, to hit the coffee shop before getting to work.

It was in the middle of the gas crises of 1978 and this was Mario's week to drive his other two passengers and Jimmy to work. Next week would be another guy's turn. That's how they had figured it out, to take turns providing transportation, since at this time in New York you could only get gas on alternate days for which the date matched the last odd or even digit of your license plate number. It was a time-consuming and confusing annoyance. Even worse, there were already cases of violence when drivers cut in line or otherwise did not follow the rules. It was an ugly time in the nation.

A gallon of unleaded regular gas was going for a price of about $ .60, to over $1.00 when it really got bad that year. It didn't matter, though, as drivers would pay any price just to get gas, or would steal it from other cars with unlocked gas caps. Locking gas caps were selling really well.

Dean and Scotty were basically captive in Mario's car; it was warm in there, and they really wanted to get moving. Unfortunately, Jimmy sometimes ran late.

Usually, Mario would ring Jimmy's doorbell, but sometimes, he just called up to him. He knew Jimmy's three children and his wife would be awake, but he didn't always know if Jimmy was awake. It was as much of a nuisance getting Jimmy as it was getting gas. But this is what they did for each other – they were co-workers and friends.

Mario had served in the Navy during Vietnam a few years earlier and Jimmy, still in his twenties, had recently served in the peace-time Army; Mario looked after his younger buddy. Mario, his wife Joan, and their two children would join Jimmy, his wife Carla and their three children once or twice a month, to shop in their neighborhood, to relax in their small backyard, to drink beer, barbeque, and watch the children play. They had been doing this for the three years that they had been working together.

Now, though, it was time to go to work. Finally, when Jimmy came out of the building. Dean and Scotty cheered.

"Hey, amigo, what's your hurry, man, we ain't got to get to work on time this morning, only if you want to lose a half-hour's pay!" Dean called out.

Mario got in behind the wheel. Jimmy climbed in the back with Scotty.

"Hey, what's up? How you guys doing?" Jimmy mumbled to everyone.

"We're okay man," Dean said. "Can't leave that woman of yours alone in bed, eh?"

"No man," Jimmy said, "I'm just tired."

"Yeah, you and me both, boy," said Scotty. He and Dean were also married with children, but they were always on time when Mario picked them up first in another section of Brooklyn, or when they picked Mario up, also in Brooklyn.

Jimmy didn't need to volunteer his car to get the crew to work since he lived so close to their jobs and was the last pick-up.

Jimmy was a boilermaker, trained on the job, though formerly serving as a mechanic in the Army. He was wiry, of English and Irish descent, and sported a thin red mustache and goatee that matched his hair color, with dark green eyes. Easy-going and friendly, he was young and even-tempered.

Mario was a welder, previously trained in the Navy several years before. He was a small but stocky Latino man, on the edge of 5'-6" with curly black hair, thick eyebrows, but clean-shaven, revealing a dark, thick face. He did not look like a man that one should get on the wrong side of, though, he was sparse in how he presented his reserved menace.

They rode from Jimmy's house to their usual coffee shop. Jimmy and Scotty got out of the car and went in to get four coffees, two buttered rolls, two doughnuts, and four egg sandwiches. Now it was on to work. A few more blocks down Flushing Avenue and they were at the Carleton Avenue gate of the Brooklyn Navy Yard.

Driving through the gate, with the parking permit card on the dashboard, and then parking the car, they walked across the lot into Building # 131.

This building contained the boiler shop, the machine shops, the tool room, and the employee's locker room, adjacent to Dry Dock # 1, the oldest dry dock in the Yard.

This was where the Civil War ship the USS MONITOR had been constructed. The USS MONITOR was the first ironclad ship of the U.S. Navy and was considered to be the first modern warship. The battleship USS MAINE (ACR-1) came out of the Brooklyn Yard, and following its sinking in Havana harbor, led directly to the Spanish-American War.

The battleship USS ARIZONA (BB-39) was launched there and remains a monument at Pearl Harbor following it's sinking on December 7, 1941. The battleship USS MISSOURI (BB-63) was built in Brooklyn, on which the documents ending WW II were signed in 1945, to mention just a few of the ships that came out of the Yard. There was no lack of history here in this place.

When the government ran the Yard during WW II, tens of thousands of workers were employed there twenty-four hours a day in three shifts. The facility was closed to servicing Navy ships in the mid-1960s; during the late 1970s, however, various private businesses occupied selected spaces in several buildings, manufacturing or creating different products, with two companies actually repairing both Navy and merchant ships, either when they were tied up to the piers, or in any one of the two or three dry docks still in operation.

Although not the glorious place that it once was, if one was observant and thought about it, this was storied, hallowed ground. Mario had realized the significance of working here, but it hadn't reached that stage of becoming a religious experience. It was a job.

Their usual day at the Yard involved working on one or more Navy ships, in cooperation with other trades, as the boilermakers rebuilt the propulsion boilers and the other trades repaired various other equipment and systems.

Mario supported the boilermakers, as well as other trades as needed, either on the ships or in any of the workshops where his services were needed. He was known far and wide as one of the best boiler welders on the East Coast.

The Navy had extremely strict specifications and testing criteria for high pressure boiler welds, able to hold back greater than at least 2,000 psi, and Mario's training and reputation were well-deserved. He was paid at a 1st Class mechanic's wage and was making good money for that time in the late '70s, at close to $9.00 per hour, roughly equating to about $25.00 per hour thirty-five years later.

The four of them went up the stairs in the building to the locker room to have their breakfast, to change into their work clothes and to clock in. There were dozens of other workers in the locker room, eating their breakfast, drinking coffee or tea, changing their clothes and talking.

There were boilermakers, machinists, welders, burners, carpenters, pipe fitters, painters, riggers, and even one old guy aged in his '70s, a former riveter, from WWII days. He never wanted to retire; he just wanted to keep on working, and would probably do so well into his '80s as long as there was work at the Yard.

Dean, Scotty, Jimmy, and most of the rest of the boiler gang were much younger than the older riveter. They were in their early twenties and thirties, and were working as many hours as they could now while the money was available from overtime. Mario was thirty-six years old and had been married for six years. Some of the other welders were about his age or younger, and some were way older and had been welding for many years.

Once they had clocked in with their time cards, each of the workers went to his or her (there were a few female welders and pipefitters) respective shops. Assignments were given by the shop supervisors to individuals or work gangs consisting of mechanics' helpers, 3rd Class, 2nd Class, and 1st Class mechanics, to be monitored at the work sites by the "snappers," the assistant supervisors. Jimmy, as a 1st Class boilermaker, would sometimes be assigned with other boilermakers to remove and replace 1" and 2" diameter tubes in selected ship's boilers, which included burning them out with a torch, then installing new ones by rolling them tight within the steel drums with a hand-held electric rolling machine. Both of these operations could kill mechanics if not performed correctly. Today, however, Jimmy, with a helper, were assigned to work on precision grinding of boiler header hand-hole gasket surfaces.

This process involved using a specialized grinding machine, stones, and a micrometer, carrying these items in a tool box that weighed about thirty pounds.

The hand holes, some dozen or so on each header, were oval-shaped openings in these steel boiler sections that provided access for removing and installing replacement tubes.

The task was to grind the seating surfaces smoothly to within .5000 of an inch tolerance on all sides of the seat. This provided for steam-tight closure when the hand hole cover plates were re-installed, using new high pressure gaskets. The plates were tightened to be leak-proof against the header with a sizable nut and dog, using a ¾ drive socket and breaker bar.

The integrity of these seating surfaces was critical to providing a sealed connection that, depending on the boiler type, would need to hold back anywhere from 600 to 1,200 pounds per square inch (psi) of steam pressure, and greater for hydrostatic testing following repairs.

Just as they were leaving the shop to walk out of the building to the ship that they were going to work on, Jimmy saw Smitty, one of the carpenters, carrying an oxy-acetylene torch past the workbench just outside of the boiler shop. Jimmy didn't think much of it at the time, although carpenters didn't usually carry torches. They were mostly used by a separate trade, the burners, who would do flame cutting for other workers as needed.

Jimmy and his helper, George, walked across the gangway from the pier to the ship, a vintage World War II destroyer. They proceeded to their job site in the after fire room, below the main deck, by walking through various passageways and climbing down several ladders. Setting up their grinding machine parallel to one of the hand holes, connecting the machine to a 100 psi air hose from a common manifold, Jimmy would then adjust the four set screws with an Allen wrench so that the stone would grind evenly on all surfaces of the opening.

They spent the morning completing six holes, between setting up, taking their allowable coffee break and then leaving the ship for lunch. They walked back to the boiler shop with the other boilermakers working on that ship, who were replacing selected one-inch tubes for each of two boilers.

When they got back to the shop, they started to eat their sandwiches, when the burner supervisor, a guy named Alvin, came in and asked, "Hey, did anyone see anybody walking around with a torch this morning?"

One of the boilermakers, Ryan, said, "Yeah, I seen a lot of guys walking around with torches, that's what some guys do around here."

"No, I'm not talking about that, I'm talking maybe somebody who wasn't a burner."

"Hey Al," said Jimmy, "I saw Smitty the carpenter with a torch this morning, what about it?"

"Thanks, that's all I needed to know," Al said, and left the shop.

"What was that all about?" another boilermaker, Bob said.

"I don't know. Anyone else know?" Jimmy asked.

"You got me," Anthony said, another boilermaker.

"I guess we'll find out," Jimmy said.

All of the boilermakers, and everyone else around the yard, finished their lunch, for which they had one-half hour, then they gathered their tools and any other materials that they needed for the afternoon's work. Then they returned the ships that they were assigned to.

Jimmy and George finished the remaining six holes on the header that they had started on that morning and moved to the second header on the other side of the boiler.

They completed two more holes before it was precisely 3:45 p.m. and time to knock off, to climb the ladders out of the fire room, to leave the ship at the gangway, to make it back to the shop, then to the time clock outside of the locker room, exactly at 4:00 p.m.

When they got back to the shop, Jimmy put the grinder box back onto one of the tool shelves where it belonged. George and he made their way out of the shop with the other boilermakers to wash up.

Not that they had any hot water for this purpose, though. The faucets serving the large trough-like sinks never dispensed anything but cold water, summer or winter. It was a particular point of contention amongst the workers, but no one in management or a union representative ever did anything about it. Basically, these guys were just on their own.

For most of the workers, coming off of the ships in the filthy condition that they did, no amount of water at any temperature would clean them up – basically, everyone just performed a perfunctory splash of ice-cold water, then changed into their street clothes, to clean up at home, and even doing that just as best as possible, until the next workday. It was a grimy business working on ships.

Jimmy met up with Mario, Dean, and Scotty for the ride home. Walking to Mario's car, Jimmy said, "That was funny about Alvin looking for that torch. I wonder what's up with that."

Mario said, "I was talking to Big Julie, one of the pipe fitters. He was telling me that some guy ripped off a torch that was laying on a work bench, but Alvin, the burner foreman, found out who took it."

"You know, the guy who told Alvin about that could be looking at some trouble from the carpenters for ratting this guy out."

Jimmy said, "Hey, man, when Alvin was asking everyone about that torch this morning, I told him that I saw Smitty walking around with one. I didn't think much about it when I told him."

"You know," Dean said, "That kind of stuff can really come back to bite you."

"Yeah," Scotty said. "That kind of talk can mess you up."

"Listen," Jimmy said, "I didn't know nothing about ripping off no torch. A guy asks me a question and I answered him."

"Alright, Jimmy," Mario said, "We'll be watching your back. Don't worry about it, yet."

"OK, but you guys got to mean it," Jimmy said.

"Yeah, yeah," Dean answered. "Don't worry, man, we got it."

Mario dropped Jimmy off at his building where they had started that morning. He took Dean and Scotty home.

Before he got out of the car, Dean said, "I don't know what's going to happen to Jimmy. I've seen this kind of thing before. Guys get mad about people talking out of turn."

"Yeah," Mario said, "But here it seems like Jimmy was just answering Alvin. He didn't know there was an agenda."

"That may be," Scotty added, "but that don't mean a thing to somebody who's feeling righteous about getting away with stealing property since no one was taking care of it – now it's up for grabs and never mind that it wasn't theirs – it's theirs now."

"Now look at us," Dean said. "We're buds with Jimmy, but Jimmy's a rat. If we take Jimmy's back, we better be watching our backs."

"Dean's right," Scotty said. "I don't know that I want to be in that spot of taking Jimmy's side against what can be a real ugly situation."

Mario was silent for awhile and just drove. Then he said, "Look, I'm not even one of you boilermakers. I'm just one of the welders that helps you guys out. But I know Jimmy. I work with the guy and we're pals. I won't be giving him to the wolves."

"That's up to you, man," Scotty said. "I don't know that I can do that."

"Me too," Dean said. "Like I said, I've seen this before when I was working at this garage that I was working at. Some guy walked off with some brake pads and somebody told the boss – I don't know why he told him, they weren't his brakes, but he ratted anyway. The rest of the gang took care of him good – put sugar in his gas tank, messed him up. It would have been dangerous to take his side. Anyone doing that could have been next on the hit list."

Scotty said, "I'm on Dean's side. We're skating on thin ice here. Jimmy did the deed. He's got to pay the price."

"Oh, yeah," Mario said, "you know what side I'm on? Jimmy's. You guys can do what you want, but I'm going to pay the price to defend him."

Dean, sitting in the front seat, looked back at Scotty. No one was comfortable. Dean was thinking about what Jimmy might be facing tomorrow – some of these guys at the Yard were morbidly territorial, even for things that didn't belong to them. It could become hazardous.

Scotty was set on minding his own business. It wasn't healthy to go against the code, not even for someone in his own shop gang.

Mario kept driving. He knew that most of the other trade Yard workers respected him. Even knowing this, he wasn't sure that he could pull this off. It was a very difficult position to be in. While it seemed that Jimmy's answer to Alvin was in complete innocence, it wasn't going to come out that way to most of the other guys – Dean and Scotty had set the tone for that reaction. Mario kept driving.

Dropping Dean off, he said, "I'm on for tomorrow's pick-up, so I'll see you in the morning."

"You know what," Dean said, "how about I take my own car tomorrow."

Scotty said, "I'll go along with Dean. I'll get myself in tomorrow."

"Okay, boys," Mario said. "You're on your own."

"Yeah, hombre," Dean said, "So are you."

Once Mario was alone in the car and continued on his way home, he thought about his decision to back Jimmy. There was no other choice for him, he resolved. He was going to stick with Jimmy, his friend and buddy.

When he arrived home, he told his wife what had happened that day. Joan knew well the quirks and codes of these trade workers along the Brooklyn waterfront. She had been married to Mario long enough and had socialized enough with different friends of Mario's, and especially, Jimmy and his family. She had been indoctrinated into the rules of these workers.

She wasn't too happy about Mario's decision to stand by Jimmy, suspecting what could be the consequences, but knew there was nothing else he could do. Even though Mario himself could be larcenous and didn't necessarily disagree with taking an unattached torch, he was unequivocal in his loyalty to Jimmy. Mario's self-reliance and sense of purpose was one of his strongest attributes.

"Here we go again," Joan said to Mario. "Another bunch of clowns mouthing off."

"It's way more than that. You know exactly how it's going. We could be headed for lots more trouble. This is starting with those guys against Jimmy, and it may get to me, but it's also going to end with me."

The next morning was just as hot as the day before. Mario drove alone to Jimmy's house. This morning, Jimmy was standing in front of his building.

"Hey, buddy, how you doing?" Mario greeted him.

"I don't know, yet, let's see what's going on when we get to work."

"You know, man, it may not turn into anything," Mario said.

"Well, like I said, I don't know," Jimmy answered.

They stopped at the coffee shop. Jimmy got out and picked up their coffee and snacks. They drove into the Yard and parked the car.

Walking their separate ways, Jimmy to the boiler shop and Mario to the welders, Mario said, "I'll see you later. Maybe I'll be on your boat today."

"Yeah, maybe. I'll see you."

When Jimmy went into the shop to pick up his grinder tool box, Dean and Scotty didn't say hello. No one said hello, except the boilermaker foreman, Johnson.

"Jimmy, don't get caught up in these knuckleheads' nonsense. I heard about Smitty and Alvin and all of that business from yesterday. Just move on, man. You have work to do." Although he was saying these words, Johnson, too, knew what could happen. People could be killed over this kind of thing.

"Okay, boss," he said. "I got it."

As he approached George to get ready to go, Johnson stopped him and said, "Jimmy, never mind George, take Phil with you today, start showing him how to grind holes."

Jimmy hesitated. George looked away and walked away. Jimmy looked at Phil, a young 3rd Class mechanic who had been with the boiler gang for just a couple of months. He was basically a helper, but had come from an iron work shop and rated 3rd Class pay. He was learning boiler work.

Jimmy felt the other guys looking at him. He wasn't feeling too well, but knew that he had to move. "Phil, you and me, let's get going," he said.

Phil stood still for a moment. Johnson had decided that morning that Phil would be working with Jimmy, since George had started talking about Jimmy, the rat, as soon as he had come into the shop.

Johnson wasn't going to put up with any dissension. If George didn't want to work with Jimmy then Johnson had to work around that – the hand holes had to get done, they were on a tight schedule for this ship, and Jimmy was really good at it.

It was as good a time as any to start getting Phil broken in on the specialized operation of grinding hand-hole seats. Johnson was hoping that nothing else was going to come of anyone turning on Jimmy. It was distracting and dangerous. Phil moved towards Jimmy. He wasn't that comfortable about working with Jimmy, now that the other guys had marked him. Phil needed this job and would have to do what Johnson told him to do, but he didn't have to like it.

As Jimmy and Phil walked out of the shop, they were not talking. Jimmy was thinking about how his innocent remark had escalated into this edgy, uncertain atmosphere.

They made their way aboard the ship and then below into the forward fire room. Getting started, Jimmy proceeded to show Phil how to set up the grinder in one hole, with the arm connected to the motor holding the stone, to grind the gasket surface in the adjacent hole.

It was not overly complicated, but the set screws that needed to be adjusted to true-up the stone perpendicular to the gasket surface required that they be turned in the opposite direction to how it intuitively felt like they needed to be turned.

It took some practice and a moderate level of mechanical feel to adjust the machine correctly, but it could be mastered.

Jimmy had been used to working with George, a quiet, calm guy who had picked up the basics of grinding holes, but wasn't overly enthusiastic about it, nor did he need to be. He just needed to assist Jimmy. Jimmy was used to working with George.

While Phil was basically quiet right now, Jimmy could sense that he was that way because he was uncomfortable about having to work with a guy that others thought of as a rat. They didn't talk much during this first morning of working together, just enough to complete two holes during the next hour.

Then, without any warning shout, a huge 2" x 8" x 6' long plank of wood came hurtling out of the overhead between the catwalk, just missing Jimmy's shoulder.

Phil dove away, Jimmy flinched – he knew he was now a target. Looking up, he couldn't see anything except some scaffolding along the side of the boiler with other planks across the steel. He didn't see any carpenters up there, but they were the ones who had installed this maze of steel and wood. It was only their shop that built these temporary structures. The carpenters always made certain that planks were secured properly and that they never fell out of the overhead by themselves. This was not a random accident – this was a calculated hit.

Jimmy figured that this was probably enough weaponry that would be used for today and went back to grinding one more hole, without saying a word to Phil.

He looked at his watch and said to Phil, "That's it for now. Let's get back to the shop for break."

"Fine with me," Phil answered.

Back at the shop after stopping at the coffee coach, Jimmy told Johnson what had happened. "Hey, boss, I just missed getting a plank driven into my skull."

"You sure about that?"

"Look, I know when scaffolding is supposed to stay put – this board came shooting right out of the overhead, aiming for me."

"This is getting out of hand," Johnson said. "I'm going to talk to Angelo, the carpenter foreman. Just because one of his guys took a torch and you just answered a question from Alvin doesn't mean one bit that this should get vicious. Everything's wrong with this and it has to stop right now."

"I'm on your side, boss. I'm on my side too, and I want to keep all of my sides, and my top, front and back as well."

"Don't worry, Jimmy. I'll take care of it."

"Okay, thanks."

But Jimmy wasn't too sure that Johnson could get this done. Sometimes people could be extremely stubborn, and completely unreasonable.

No one else in the boiler shop talked to Jimmy. Everyone finished their coffee break talking to each other, or not talking at all. He collected Phil and they walked back to the ship. The rest of the afternoon was uneventful. Phil and he continued grinding hand holes with Jimmy providing instructions until knock-off time. They dismantled the grinding machine, placed it in the tool box and walked back to the shop. It was over for today.

Jimmy met Mario at the parking lot. "Jimmy, man, I heard all about you almost buying it today," Mario said.

"Yeah, it was close, but I still live. It must have been the carpenters, maybe even Smitty himself," Jimmy said. "Johnson said he was going to talk to Angelo at the carpenters and maybe we can end this thing right now. I'm not looking forward to tomorrow and maybe getting killed again."

"This is bad, my brother," said Mario. "Maybe Johnson can take care of it, but you know how it is, Smitty may just keep this going. Listen, I need to take my son to a doctor's appointment tomorrow for his check-up. Joan has to be at work. I won't be coming in, so you've got to get here on your own."

"Alright, Mario, I'll make it, I'll take my car for a change," Jimmy answered.

"Okay, you hang in there; maybe this is just all over after today."

"You never know, maybe," Jimmy said. It didn't seem to either one of them that this would end it though.

The next morning Jimmy picked up coffee and a doughnut, then drove to work.

He walked to the locker room. Changing his clothes and making some small talk with a few of the other guys who seemed neutral or who didn't know anything about the challenges of the past two days, he finished his coffee and went down the stairs to the boiler shop.

Only Johnson, already there, said hello to him. The rest of the boiler gang didn't say anything. It was eerie. Just two days before everything was just fine. Now this was a very treacherous place to be working.

Phil and he picked up their gear, then headed to the machine shop at the other side of the building. Some of the stones were worn down from grinding on the steel of the hand hole seats and needed to be dressed up, cut on a lathe to provide a sharp, fresh angle.

Jimmy had to have this done every few days, whenever he needed sharp stones again, and he could just stop at any one of the lathe operator's stations who would cut the stones.

"Morning, Stuffy, how about dressing up some stones for me?" Jimmy said to one of the lathe guys that he knew, a short, portly man, hence his nickname.

"Hey, Jimmy, how you doing? I usually see you with George, who's this guy?" he asked.

"This here is Phil. He's only been with us boilermakers for a few months, but we're paired up today for me to show him the ropes," Jimmy said.

"Okay, good deal. Let me dress up those stones; it'll only take me a couple of minutes."

There wasn't any rat opinion here, thought Jimmy. Stuffy was a friendly and helpful guy. Stuffy finished cutting six stones and handed them back to Jimmy, who put them back in the tool box.

"Thanks, Stuffy, this helps a lot."

"Anytime, kid," he said. Phil and he walked away, out of the building and then to the ship. They worked on a couple of holes, with Phil setting up one of them, grinding for a few passes, with Jimmy coaching. It looked like Phil would get it, then he could be up for a promotion to 2nd Class mechanic, with a modest hourly pay raise.

They left the ship for coffee break. Phil and he were talking a little more. Phil seemed to be adjusting to working with a perceived stool pigeon. Jimmy was just waiting for the other shoe to drop, though. He didn't know if Johnson had talked to Angelo, nor if Smitty had given up the torch that he had taken, without a fight.

Lunch was a quiet affair, and the rest of the afternoon was just as quiet, except for the whining noise of the grinding stones against steel and the other sounds of mechanics working in the fire room

The relative calm was broken later when he went to the parking lot at the end of the work day and Jimmy saw the condition of the headlights on his car – both headlights were smashed, shards of glass were spread out in front of the car.

Jimmy stared at them for a few seconds. It was difficult to look at, but he couldn't help it. At least they didn't try to smash him directly today. He drove home.

Fortunately it was summer and still light enough to drive. He wouldn't need his headlights right away and could get them fixed over the weekend, but it would be expensive.

His wife Carla started shaking when Jimmy told her what happened. He called Mario and told him what happened.

"I'll pick you up tomorrow to go to work," Mario told him. "It doesn't sound like Johnson had that talk with Angelo, so you know what? I'm going to have a talk with Angelo and maybe Smitty himself tomorrow," Mario told Jimmy.

"You're going to do that?" Jimmy said.

"Yeah, I'm going to do that – there won't be anymore of this going down, man."

"I could talk to Smitty tomorrow," Jimmy said.

"No, I don't thinks so. I don't think that would be a good idea – Smitty is not going to listen to anything you have to say – he is a blameless criminal and I don't think you're going to reach him. But he will listen to me," Mario said.

"How's that going to happen?" Jimmy asked.

"Because," Mario said, "Smitty is going to understand that if he doesn't listen to what I have to say, then he is going to have his ears welded shut to his head and he won't have anything to listen to anymore."

"You know, my man, you're right – Smitty has to hear this from someone else, not from me. If you would do this for me, then I'm your friend for life," Jimmy said.

"Jimbo, you already my friend for life. This means we got to make sure you stay alive!"

"I'm right there with you on that, man. I'll see you in the morning – I'll be right out front, on time," said Jimmy.

"Okay, I'll see you then."

The next morning Mario came by and picked up Jimmy. Coffee purchased, then into the Yard and upstairs. They parted company out of the locker room.

Mario called the carpenter shop from a phone in the welding shop. "Let me talk to Angelo," he said. He waited a moment.

"Angelo here."

"Listen, this is Mario the welder. I need to stop by your shop for a minute before I head out – will you be there in the next couple of minutes?"

"Yeah," he answered. "Come on by."

Mario walked into the carpenter's shop in the next building over from the welders. Angelo was there, so were Smitty and several of the other carpenters, getting ready to leave for their assignments.

"Angelo, let me talk to you privately for a minute," Mario said.

"Why don't you just tell me what's on your mind, Mario?" he said.

Mario hesitated for a second, but it was just as well. The other carpenters, and especially Smitty, needed to hear what he had to say.

"Well, it's like this, one of my buddies in the boiler shop, Jimmy, told Alvin that he saw a guy that had a torch. This friend of mine didn't think about what that torch was doing in that guy's hands, he just answered Alvin. Now, seems like there's something going on to get back at my buddy for ratting the torch guy out. A couple of dicey things happened to my friend yesterday." He paused. "I want to tell you that you need to tell your guys that this isn't going to go on today, or the next day, or anytime."

Mario stood still, looking straight at Angelo. He didn't even glance at the other carpenters.

"Well, now let me tell you something, Mario," Angelo started, "If this rat guy is a friend of yours, then you must be a rat too. I'm going to ask you to leave this shop right now, before something bad happens to you." Angelo stared at Mario. The carpenters stared at both of them.

"I guess I didn't get my point across," Mario continued. "If that's your read on this, then I don't have anything more to say."

"That's right, you got nothing more to say," Angelo said.

Mario didn't move for just a moment, processing the fact that even this shop foreman didn't get it. He turned around, looked from Angelo to Smitty, and said, "I'll be seeing you, man."

Mario walked out of the shop. He was not a happy man, but he was now determined to make sure that Smitty, and everyone else, would get the point that there wasn't going to be any more actions taken against Jimmy, or himself.

Nothing else happened to either Jimmy or Mario during the rest of the day. Mario was telling Jimmy what happened at the carpenters as they walked to the parking lot in the late afternoon to go home.

They both saw it at the same time - the windshield wipers on Mario's car were missing and the wiper arms were bent and twisted back; they were no longer functional.

This is what you get for standing up for your friend, thought Mario. It's going to cost me some money to get those arms replaced. Now it's war.

"Look what they did!" Jimmy cried. "This is insane, we've got to get these guys. I guess Johnson never made that call to Angelo and your talk with him really didn't go over at all," he went on.

"Yeah, I guess not, like I told you. But I have a plan for Smitty. It's time for me to get tough with that slimy meatball. I will take care of him as soon as I have the right situation."

"Don't you want me there with you?" Jimmy asked.

"No, I got this – no one is going to mess with me or one of my buds. On second thought, maybe you and I can work together tomorrow on welding those tube ends. Johnson told me he needed me to do that."

"Alright, Mario, I'll be with you and you let me know if you want me to do anything – I'm a former Army guy. I can kill guys just as good as you," Jimmy said.

"It's okay," Mario answered. "My Navy days are behind me too, but maybe I won't have to actually kill the guy. This won't go on much longer. I just need Smitty in the right place."

The next day, before Mario went to the welding shop, he asked Johnson to call his boss Gary, the welding foreman, and tell him that Mario was needed to weld new u-bend tube ends on one of the economizer bundles at the top of one of the boilers. Gary didn't think much about this. The boilermakers asked for Mario whenever they needed him for precision welding, and depending on scheduling, Gary sent him over.

Mario entered the boiler shop and asked Johnson, "What's the ship, what boiler needs welding?"

"We're starting on the JOHN T. EVERSON, dry dock three, for the 2A boiler economizer on the upper level in after fire room," Johnson answered.

"Okay, then how about instead of having Jimmy work on hand holes today, he fits those tube ends for me to weld?" Mario asked.

"Alright by me. I'll have Phil pair up with Manny to work on door gaskets," Johnson answered.

Then he said, "Jimmy, you're on with Mario this morning welding u-bends."

"Fine by me," Jimmy said. He went to the tool room and took a pneumatic grinder, two lengths of hose, some couplings, and a foot-long straight edge, along with his own converted welding rod can with his three-pound hammer, 12-inch adjustable wrench, extension ruler and other tools. On the way out he took the canvas bag filled with about a dozen steel u-bend tube ends for that boiler.

Mario said to Jimmy, "First, let Johnson make a phone call." He said to Johnson, "I need you to call Angelo. I'm going to need a carpenter to set up some scaffolding there. Have Angelo send Smitty. I want him to work on this."

Mario's tone was perfectly even and didn't reveal any other motive, though Johnson and Jimmy could guess that Mario knew just what he needed to do with Smitty.

Johnson picked up the shop phone and dialed the carpenters. "Angelo, it's Johnson," he said.

"We're going to need some angle iron and planking for scaffolding behind 2B boiler on the upper level in the after fire room of the EVERSON this morning. We're welding economizer u-bends. I need Smitty to meet my guys to scope it out back there."

"I need him in about an hour. Can you make that happen?"

"Sure, Johnson, I'll get him over there for you," Angelo said.

"That's great. Thanks."

Jimmy and Mario left the boiler shop and walked to the pier where the EVERSON was berthed. They worked their way below to the fire room. Mario grabbed the welding cable connected to the machine on the pier. Jimmy connected his hoses to a compressed air manifold set up for mechanics to use as needed.

They climbed onto the upper level catwalk behind 2B boiler, at the boiler economizer tube bank. These tubes, filled with water when the boiler was in operation, were in the path of the hot combustion gasses exiting the firebox. This would pre-heat the water to assist in reaching the approximately 500 ^{0} F temperature required to convert it to steam under the boiler's operating pressure once the feed water entered the steam drum. The tube return ends required welds that were completely fail-safe.

Jimmy placed the first u-bend into two tube ends. He pulled it out, put on his goggles and grinded each of the ends to make a better fit. Now using his straight edge, he leveled the u-bend and had Mario tack weld each side.

Checking for level again, he had Mario continue to complete the welds. Then, they fitted and welded three more sets. Later, the Navy boiler inspector would x-ray the welds; Mario's welds never failed.

Before they left, however, they heard someone walking towards the rear of the boiler. Smitty, the carpenter torch thief, turned the corner and stopped short.

"Hey, I didn't know it was you that Angelo told me to meet here, and sure not your rat buddy, Jimmy," he said. Mario and Jimmy turned to face Smitty.

"Well, I'll tell you what, here is what I need you to do," Mario said to Smitty. "You are going to quit right this second of doing anything else to Jimmy, either to his person, to anything he owns, or to any tools he's using, or to anyone he's working with," he said sharply.

"Now you wait a second, my man," Smitty snapped back. "Jimmy is a rat. He told Alvin that I glommed a torch. That was no business of Jimmy's to tell anyone about anything what I do, you understand that? If you're still jumping in here, then maybe somebody needs to keep teaching you a lesson in minding your own business. How would you like me to take care of you some more, too? Maybe have a plank fall out of the overhead on you? How would you like to be known as a rat pal?"

Mario didn't move, neither did Jimmy. There wasn't anyone that Jimmy could recall who spoke to Mario like that, and no one usually did it again.

Mario wasn't a very big man, but he did have a reputation for not backing down from anything, and could be violent when he needed to be. Although Jimmy was a little milder, he too, would stand up for himself as necessary. Working down here on the waterfront, in these ships, had steeled these men to difficult circumstances.

"Smitty, being a pal to a rat is not what I am going to be known as," Mario said. "What I am going to be known as is the guy who electrocuted a carpenter who was a thief, a liar, and a bully. Now I am going to tell you only one more time, which you have to understand, is that if you do one more thing to Jimmy, or to me, then even if you come at me with a claw hammer, I am going to either electrocute you with this welding rig or I will beat you to death with the handle."

"And Jimmy here, he will grind your face to small pieces of meat with his machine and then he will smash those pieces with his lump hammer. You got that, man?"

Mario lifted his welding clip handle with a steel rod in it to chest height in front of Smitty ready to lunge straight at him. Mario knew his rod wouldn't electrocute Smitty just by touching his clothing, but Smitty didn't know that.

Jimmy, picking up on Mario's lead, lifted the grinder in front of him with both hands. He punched and released the trigger starting the carbide blade spinning for a moment at its screaming top speed.

Smitty's eyes opened wide. He stepped back away from these menaces. He hadn't thought that Mario and Jimmy would be having this confrontation with him.

Smitty, although a stocky man himself, couldn't take the chance that these two guys would certainly carry through with their threats. He hadn't figured on Jimmy having back-up. This fight wasn't worth it, waiting to see if Mario would kill him defending his friend, or if Jimmy would cut him up defending himself, or defending his friend. The acts of destruction were over as far as Smitty was concerned. Visibly shaken, Smitty said, "Okay, Mario. I'm done."

"Good answer," Mario said. "Glad we could come to an agreement. You made the right choice."

Smitty turned and disappeared around the side of the boiler. Mario and Jimmy looked at each other.

"Thanks, man, that was really smooth," Jimmy said.

"Only to the point, Jimmy. It's just what needed to be said to get this stopped."

"Well, now it's back to work," Jimmy said. "We've got lots of tubes to fit. Let's see what we can get done before break."

At break, they climbed out of the fire room to the weather deck, and then across the brow onto the pier. They stopped at the coffee coach, and then went to the boiler shop.

Word had already gotten around. George said a mild hello to Jimmy, and so did some of the other boilermakers. The reign of terror had passed.

Quitting time at days end, Mario and Jimmy met in the locker room to change from their work clothes. They went to Mario's car and drove out of the Yard.

"Not bad, quiet today, except for the interruption for conflict resolution," Mario said.

"Yeah," Jimmy said. "Just another day in the pit to earn a dollar. I'm glad you had your little chat with Smitty, and that I was with you."

"Yeah," Mario said, "We definitely got his attention. He saw the light – no more messing around with revenge."

"That's great, I really appreciate it. You came through for me, my pal." Jimmy said.

"It's nothing, mi amigo. Like you say, just another day on the line, getting paid, or paying out."

About the Author

Larry Samuels currently lives on the Eastern Shore of Maryland with his wife of twenty-seven years, Marguerite, who is an adjunct professor of English at a university as well as holding a position as an advocate for academically at-risk students at a community college. They have two teenage children, Paul and Rebecca.

Formerly a resident of New York City, he spent his youth and adult life moving many times, counting fourteen addresses as of this writing. He was in the Boy Scouts, played handball in schoolyards, stickball and other games in the streets, and worked at many part-time jobs in his neighborhoods, since the age of thirteen. Following high school graduation, and taking a selection of college courses, filling-in with several part-time jobs, he left school and worked as a taxicab driver throughout the city before joining the Navy during Vietnam.

While on four years' active service, he achieved the rate of E-5 / Petty Officer 2nd Class, operating and repairing high-pressure steam plants, on a guided missile destroyer in the Gulf of Tonkin, and then on a destroyer escort along the coast of Africa, in the Middle East and through the Suez Canal. Having traveled extensively during this time, his writings reflect the emotional elements of these military experiences, interwoven with adversity, social relationships, and cultural history during wartime, and as a civilian.

Receiving an Honorable Discharge, he then held several positions in mechanical technology, including three years on the Brooklyn waterfront rebuilding ships' boilers, and for a year as a licensed operating engineer in a commercial refrigeration plant.

Returning to college under the GI Bill, after graduating he worked in several technical capacities, until he secured his career position as a facilities manager providing administrative services, and performing capital construction coordination for a multi-building municipal public library system. He retired after twenty-seven years with the organization.

During this time, as a dad, he served as a Cub Scout leader, as an adult Scout leader trainer, and as a Sunday school teacher along with Marguerite, in addition to serving in several capacities at his church.

Although now retired from the library, he is currently employed as a substitute teacher for the local county public school system in grades pre-kindergarten through high school.

He is also involved in his community, volunteering as a reading tutor in the elementary schools, as a youth character development coach, on the Board of Directors of a youth sports and academic program, and on the Board of a non-profit organization providing services and advocacy for adults challenged with mental illness.

He serves as a member of a local racial diversity action group, as a member of the National Association for the Advancement of Colored People (NAACP), on the committee restoring an historic African-American church, and as a volunteer at a Grand Army of the Republic American Legion Post established by black Civil War veterans, one of only two such posts remaining in the nation, and maintains membership in several veterans organizations.

He is also involved in several leadership roles at his own historic church, including that of Junior Warden, Cemetery Warden, Property Committee Chair, Usher, Sunday school teacher, and participates in the church's monthly Hispanic Parish dinner outreach.

In addition, he is a member of two local writers groups that promotes the fundamentals of fiction and non-fiction expression, and the development of advanced projects, of which this collection was a direct result. He was a contributing author, along with Marguerite, to a collection of prose and poetry published by one of the groups, and was a contributing editor for a member's publication of a non-fiction work.

Still working on revising several of his previously written stories, and writing new ones, he is pleased to continue being creative and productive in his writing, to share in family activities, and to participate in community service initiatives.

Appendix

Service Related Locations Visited / Ports of Call

Chronological Order: 1971 - 1975

North America – 1971 - 1972

<u>United States</u>

St. Albans Medical Facility, Queens, New York
Fort Hamilton, Brooklyn, New York
Camp Barry Naval Training Center, Great Lakes, Illinois
Waukegan, Illinois
Chicago, Illinois
Milwaukee, Wisconsin
Menominee Falls, Wisconsin
Hammond, Indiana
Philadelphia Naval Yard, Philadelphia, Pennsylvania
San Francisco, California
Travis Air Force Base, Fairfield, California
Honolulu, Hawaii
Naval Air Station, Agana, Guam

Locations / Ports (cont.)

<u>Asia</u> – 1972 - 1974

<u>Japan</u>

Naval Air Station, Tachikawa

Naval Base, Yokosuka

Yokohama

Shimoda

Okinawa

Sasebo

Beppu

Ofuna

Mt. Fuji, Shizuoka

Tokyo

Kamakura

Kure

Hiroshima

Hakodate

<u>Taiwan</u>

Taipai

Kaohsiung

Keelung

Locations / Ports (cont.)

Asia (cont.)

China

Hong Kong
Wan Chai
Aberdeen
Kowloon
New Territories

Korea

Pusan
Chinhae

Philippines

Clark Air Base, Subic Bay
Olongapo City
Manila

Vietnam

Gulf of Tonkin
Da Nang Harbor

Locations / Ports (cont.)

Caribbean

San Juan, Puerto Rico
Hamilton, Bermuda

Africa & Middle East – 1974 - 1975

Dakar, Senegal
Monrovia, Liberia
Mocamedes, Angola
Mombasa, Kenya
Assab, Ethiopia
Djibouti, French Territory of the Afars & Isaas
Bahrain Island
Hodeidah, Yemen
Socotra Island, Yemen
Muscat, Oman
Karachi, Pakistan
Bandar Abbas, Iran
Jiddah, Saudi Arabia
Suez City, Egypt
Suez Canal
Port Said, Egypt

Locations / Ports (cont.)

Europe - 1975

Rota, Spain

North America – 1975

United States

Charleston, South Carolina
Summerville, South Carolina
Columbia, South Carolina

Ships Served: Active Sea Duty – 1972 - 1975

USS PARSONS (DDG-33)
Guided Missile Destroyer - Commissioned 1959
Homeported – Yokosuka, Japan

USS TRIPPE (DE / FF-1075)
Destroyer Escort / Fast Frigate - Commissioned 1970
Homeported – Charleston, South Carolina

Ships Repaired: Brooklyn Navy Yard – 1977 - 1980

USS CALOOSAHATCHEE (AO-98)
Fleet Oiler – Commissioned 1945

USS CORRY (DD-817)
Destroyer – Commissioned 1946

USS SURIBACHI (AK-21)
Ammunition Ship – Commissioned 1956

USS GARCIA (DE-1040)
Destroyer Escort – Commissioned 1964

Ships Repaired (cont.)

USS LASALLE (LPD-3 / AGF-3)
Amphibious Transport / Command Ship – Commissioned 1964

USS JOSEPH HEWES (DE / FF-1078)
Destroyer Escort / Fast Frigate – Commissioned 1971

USS KALAMAZOO (AOR-6)
Fleet Oiler – Commissioned 1973

USS MOINESTER (DE / FF-1097)
Destroyer Escort / Fast Frigate – Commissioned 1974

Naval Boilers Operated & Repaired

Babcock & Wilcox
Combustion Engineering
Foster Wheeler

Service Record & Awards

E-3 / Fireman - E-5 / Petty Officer 2nd Class:
Boiler Tender (BT) - Shipboard High Pressure Steam Plant Operator

National Defense Medal
Vietnam Service Medal
Vietnam Campaign Medal
Combat Action Ribbon
Meritorious Unit Commendation
Good Conduct Medal
Letter of Commendation
Honorable Discharge
Golden Shellback

Veterans Group Memberships

Tin Can Sailors Association
Destroyer Escort Sailors Association
Vietnam Veterans of America

www.ingramcontent.com/pod-product-compliance
Lightning Source LLC
Chambersburg PA
CBHW030156200626
46812CB00017B/2148